W9-ATG-415

MINNESOTA AVENUE &
BENNING ROAD

Strebor on the Streetz

MINNESOTA AVENUE & BENNING ROAD

A NOVEL BY

HARELL

STREBOR BOOKS

NEW YORK   LONDON   TORONTO   SYDNEY

Strebor Books
P.O. Box 6505
Largo, MD 20792
http://www.streborbooks.com

ISBN 978-1-59309-356-3
ISBN 978-1-4516-0802-1 (ebook)
LCCN 2010940497

First Strebor Books trade paperback edition April 2012

Cover design: www.mariondesigns.com
Cover photograph: © Keith Saunders/Marion Designs

10 9 8 7 6 5 4 3 2 1

Manufactured in the United States of America

For information regarding special discounts for bulk purchases, please contact Simon & Schuster Special Sales at 1-866-506-1949 or business@simonandschuster.com

The Simon & Schuster Speakers Bureau can bring authors to your live event. For more information or to book an event, contact the Simon & Schuster Speakers Bureau at 1-866-248-3049 or visit our website at www.simonspeakers.com.

ACKNOWLEDGMENTS

First and foremost, I have to thank my Lord and Savior for blessing me with a vivid imagination and the gift to express it through written word. I am a living testimony that through You, ALL things are possible.

I have to thank my mother, Anna, for being not only my mother but also my friend. Also, I want to thank my father, Harold, for always supporting me in all that I do. Without each of you, I definitely wouldn't be the man I am today.

To my brother, JD, and my sister, Shante...always know that your big brother has your back.

To my family, I love each and every one of you from aunts and uncles to nieces and nephews and cousins. People don't know about the Milner family.

I want to thank my children for just being the joy in my life: Tre, RaShawn, Malik, Yhanae and my new addition, Charles. I work so hard so that one day none of you will have to. Everything I do in life is for you. I love you more than I love myself. You are the true definition of unconditional love. Each day you show me how blessed I truly am.

I have to thank my literary family starting with Zane. You are one of the first people to ever believe in my writing and the first to give me the opportunity and platform to share my talent with the world. You've always been very supportive, no matter how late I've been on a project. Charmaine Parker, man, you are the hardest-working woman in show business. The entire Strebor family, thanks to all of you. To the other authors that I have the pleasure of calling my friends, Darrien Lee, Tina Brooks McKinney, Allison Hobbs, Shelley Halima, La Jill Hunt and the fabulous Nikki Turner, keep blazing your own trail and setting the literary world on fire!

Finally, to all my readers, I want to thank you for your support. The love you show me doesn't go unnoticed. You are the best and I will forever be your biggest fan!

Derrick rolled over and looked at the clock. The time read 4:53 a.m. He started to panic. He was past late. He should've been up, dressed and getting ready to walk out of the door so he could get to the bus stop in time. Instead, he was still comfortably lying in his bed. Without hesitation, Derrick quickly jumped up out of the bed.

There was no way he could be late to work again. His supervisor had made that perfectly clear the last time Derrick had waltzed into the office at 6:35 a.m., five minutes late. He told Derrick then that the next time he came in late, he might as well not come in at all since he surely would be fired.

Derrick rushed into the bathroom to wash up. There wasn't enough time for him to take a shower. That time was lost earlier when he'd continued to sleep the morning away instead of getting up when his alarm clock first went off. At this point, every second was precious time needed if he was going to make it to the bus stop in time enough to catch the bus.

"Damn, do you have to be that loud?" Thomas, Derrick's roommate, said as he stood at the doorway of the bathroom. Derrick rushed past him after he finished brushing his teeth and back into his bedroom.

"Shit, my bad! I didn't mean to be loud. I'm trying to rush and get out of here. I overslept again and I can't be late anymore."

Derrick grabbed his pants and shirt and started to put them on.

"Yeah, yeah, whatever! Can you at least try to keep the noise to a minimum so a brotha can get some sleep? I don't have to get up any time soon; I was trying to enjoy the rest."

"Rub it in, why don't you? Don't worry; I'm done so you can go ahead back to sleep. I'll get up with you later on tonight or something," Derrick said as he buttoned up the last button on his shirt.

Thomas shook his head. "Damn, you're not even going to iron that or nothing? Just throw it on and head out the door, huh, man? Your mother taught you better!"

"I have no problem with ironing my clothes. Shoot, if you like, I can go back in the room and put on another outfit. And then I can head to the office and clean out my desk after I've been fired so you can handle the rent and shit by yourself, or I can go to work wrinkled, make it on time, and keep my job. You tell me, which would you prefer?"

Thomas grabbed Derrick's keys off the top of the dresser and threw them at him. With one hand, Derrick caught them.

"Have a great wrinkled day at work," Thomas replied.

Derrick laughed. "That's what I thought."

Derrick grabbed his coat, sprinted past Thomas to the front door, and headed down the steps of his apartment complex. Once he was outside, Derrick sprinted up Minnesota Avenue to the bus stop at the corner of Minnesota Avenue and Benning Road. He only had a matter of seconds left before the bus came and was on its way.

Nearly out of breathe, Derrick finally reached an empty bus stop only to see the back of his bus heading down the street.

"Shit!" Derrick yelled out of frustration.

Time was steadily ticking away and Derrick didn't know what

to do. The next bus wouldn't be there for another ten minutes or so. Predicting traffic in the D.C. area was nearly impossible to do. If traffic was light, Derrick could wait for the next bus to arrive and catch that one. It would get him to work with more than enough time. But if there was an accident, any construction or delays, or any setbacks causing traffic to be heavy, those ten minutes could add anywhere from twenty minutes to an hour and fifteen minutes to his commute and he would be late. Timing was everything.

Derrick thought about walking to the Minnesota Avenue subway station to the cab stand. It wasn't that far of a walk; only three blocks away. If there was a taxi waiting, then he could hop in. That seemed like the best option.

Derrick checked his pockets to see how much cash he had on him; eleven dollars. That was nowhere near enough. He had no other choice but to wait for the next bus and pray that God would be on his side and get him to work on time.

Derrick wanted to be prepared for the worst, in case he didn't make it on time and was late. It couldn't hurt to have a good excuse at the ready. Maybe if he could think of one good enough, his supervisor would cut him a little slack. Anything was possible and anything was better than nothing. With the way the economy and job market were, if he lost his job, Derrick realized there was no telling when he'd find another one.

It wasn't as if Derrick wasn't qualified or lacked the education to obtain one. It was hard to find anything in today's economy. Derrick could always resort to hustling on the street to get by until he found another job. Though he was raised in the ghetto, his mother didn't bring him up with the street mindset. Growing up, she made sure that she kept him as far away from the street corners and drug gangs as possible. She was the only one who raised him and not the streets.

Consumed by everything racing through his mind, Derrick didn't even notice the two men across the street from him until two gunshots rang out, breaking him from his brief daze. Derrick's survival instincts jumped in quickly and before he even knew it, he was laying on the ground, searching for cover. Everyone who grew up in the ghetto understood one thing: fired shots had intended targets, but stray bullets had everyone's name on them. There was no way he was going to allow his name to be on any of them.

Everything went silent after the first two shots. Derrick picked up his head to survey the scene. He noticed a man on the ground, apparently shot. He was trying to crawl away from the gunman. Everything in Derrick told him to get up and run but his body wouldn't listen to his mind. He continued to lie there and watch everything unfold.

The gunman walked over to the injured man and stood over him. He fired two more shots, this time into the back of the wounded man's head, instantly killing him. Derrick couldn't believe what he'd witnessed. The man had been executed right in front of him.

The streets were bare. There wasn't a police car, or even a person in sight. Derrick started to panic. It was only a matter of time before the gunman would see him and make him the next victim. Derrick got up off the ground and started to run toward the vacant shopping mall behind him. He was out in the open so his chances to escape were slim, but that was a chance he'd have to take.

The gunman noticed Derrick trying to flee the scene. In an effort to stop him, the gunman opened fire on Derrick. Gunshots hit everything from parked cars to the buildings in front of Derrick, but none of them hit him. The gunman gave chase. Derrick ran behind the shopping mall and headed for a gate leading to someone's backyard. If he stayed on the main street trying to get away, the chances of him living were minimal.

As they both ran, shots continued to ring out. It seemed as if each shot got closer and closer to hitting Derrick. Once he jumped over the first gate, the gunshots ceased. That didn't stop Derrick from running. Once he was in the neighborhood, he noticed the gunman was no longer chasing him; however, he wasn't sure what the gunman's next move was. He needed to stay two steps ahead.

Derrick headed to the Minnesota Avenue subway station. He decided to forget about work, jump on the train, and get as far away from the gunman and scene as he possibly could. Once he was safe, then he'd sort out his next move. Derrick started to cross the street to go to the subway station when he noticed the gunman walking around by the front entrance to the station.

Derrick quickly ducked behind a parked car, hoping the gunman didn't spot him. He poked his head around the car. The gunman stood there, waiting like he sensed that Derrick was close by, trying escape by getting on the train.

Derrick noticed the V8 Metro bus entering the parking lot. The gunman turned and headed into the station. There was no way he would be able to get on the train and escape. The bus was his only option to get away. Derrick darted across the street and hopped on the bus. He found a seat and crouched over so he wouldn't be detected. All he needed was for the gunman to figure out that he was on the bus, follow him, and wait for him to get off the bus. Then what would he do?

It seemed as if the bus was sitting there for hours. The gunman came out of the station and walked toward it, but didn't get on. He simply stood there. The bus driver closed the door, the bus pulled off, and headed down Minnesota Avenue back toward Benning Road.

As the bus passed the original scene of the crime, Derrick noticed a small crowd now around the body of the slain man. He couldn't help but to wonder where those same people were when the crime was first being committed. There still were no police cars in sight but it was obvious it wouldn't be long before they'd be on the scene.

In a perfect world, Derrick would've been able to wait for them to arrive and tell the police all that he'd witnessed, but Derrick didn't live in a perfect world. He lived in the real world and in the real world, all it would take would be for the gunman to make his way back down to the scene, spot him, and there would be two bodies lying on the pavement instead of one. There was no way Derrick was going to take that chance. The bus continued down the street and on to safety.

2

Police tape outlined Minnesota Avenue and Benning Road, stopping any pedestrians from contaminating the crime scene. The coroner was inspecting the body while investigators and uniformed officers canvassed the area, searching for clues and talking to possible witnesses.

Detective Peterson's car pulled up to the scene. As he got out of the car, an investigator was already approaching him. "What do we have here, Lewis?" Detective Peterson asked.

"A Hispanic male, in his mid-to-late twenties, with four gunshot wounds. He took one in the leg, one in the shoulder, and two to the head; execution-style."

"A hired hit? That's interesting."

"That's the way it's looking; this definitely wasn't a mugging or a robbery. The victim still had over five hundred dollars in his pocket."

The two of them continued to approach the body. The inspector continued, "By the shell casings, it looks like the victim tried to flee. The first shot probably hit him in the shoulder, then the second in the leg. He went down around here and was able to crawl to here, when the assailant finished off the job."

"Have we been able to identify the body?"

"No, he didn't have any ID on him."

Detective Peterson knelt down next to the body and pulled back the sheet covering him.

"Wow!" he exclaimed.

"You know him?" Investigator Lewis asked.

Detective Peterson stood back up in amazement. He couldn't believe who was lying in front of him.

"What! What is it? Who is he?" Lewis asked.

"Does the name Omar Benitez ring a bell?"

"Of course, he runs the Eastside Riderz gang. Why? This damn sure isn't him," Lewis replied.

"You're right; it's not. It's his nephew, Jose Benitez, and he's one of Omar's top lieutenants."

Investigator Lewis didn't say a word. All he could do was look at Detective Peterson with a blank stare.

Detective Peterson added, "Exactly!"

Lewis said, "Omar's going to want blood the minute he finds out his nephew was murdered."

"And he has the power to get that and more. He won't simply kill whoever killed his nephew. No, he'll kill their entire family while the killer watches it. Then he's going to torture him to death. We definitely can't beat our feet with this one. We need to get on top of this immediately. Are there any witnesses?"

"Just about everyone heard the gunshots but no one witnessed the murder, or the murderer. According to everyone, by the time they got to the scene, there was no one here."

"That's not surprising. Okay, well, we still need to interview anyone who heard the shots. Confirm what they heard and didn't see with what we know and hopefully, one thing will trigger something even better. It's definitely tree-shaking time."

"Do you really think that's going to help? Even if someone did see something, there's no way they don't realize who was killed. They recognize what's about to go down. Information about Benitez's murder is worth way more to Omar and someone definitely will be willing to sell it to him. They aren't going to tell us shit; that much we both know," Lewis said.

"Detective, we have something over here!" one of the other officers yelled.

Detective Peterson turned and walked toward the officer.

"Please tell me that it's good news. That's all I'm taking right now. What's up? What do you have?" Detective Peterson said as he was approaching the officer.

"There are more shell casings over here."

"Are they different casings?"

"No, they're the same. The way they're all scattered; check it out."

Detective Peterson looked at the pattern. The clues pointed toward the bus stop where Derrick had witnessed the murder.

Detective Peterson walked across the street to the bus stop and surveyed the area. Lewis was right behind him. Detective Peterson noticed fresh footprints leading toward the shopping center.

"What is it?" Lewis asked.

"We might've caught a break. This is what the murderer was shooting at."

"What?"

"We've got a witness. The shooter must not have noticed him at first. He was probably concentrating on the target. Then, after he dropped the target, he spotted the witness and went after him," Detective Peterson replied. "He must've been standing right here when it happened, dropped down for cover until the gunman noticed him, and then ran toward the shopping center to get away."

"But why would he be standing here this early in the morning? That doesn't make any sense."

"Yes, it does. Look where we are." Detective Peterson pointed to the bus stop. "He was waiting for his bus and probably saw the entire thing. Officer, I need you to expand the canvass to the shopping center. Let me know if you see any signs of blood, or a body. If not, then our witness got away and is on the loose."

The officers headed toward the shopping center as Detective Peterson ordered. He then continued, "Lewis, once we have a time of death narrowed down, I want the bus drivers for the X2 that operate around that time. If he was here waiting for the bus this early, more than likely he lives in the area and catches the bus regularly to work."

"No problem; I'm on it!"

"We need to find him immediately."

"Do you think he has any idea what he's in the middle of?" Lewis asked.

"My guess is no, but once word hits the street that Jose Benitez is dead, he'll know exactly how serious things are. Also, try to keep this as hush as possible. You know how fast word travels around here."

"I know, I know. Don't worry, I'm on it," Lewis said, and then walked off.

Detective Peterson walked back over to the body as it was being bagged and wheeled away. He noticed a car pulling up and walked over to it.

As the guy was getting out of the car, Detective Peterson said, "Damn, word really does travel fast!"

"What did you say?" the gentleman asked.

"Nothing."

"I hear Jose Benitez was murdered. Lay it down for me. Where are we with things?" Captain Ross asked.

"We just might, possibly, have a drug or turf war on our hands. I'm not sure yet. What I do know is that Jose Benitez was killed execution-style; my guess, a hired hit."

"So what makes you think it's a turf war?"

"I'm not sure but last night, one of the Trinidad and Montello Avenue Crew members was gunned down outside of a local carry-out and now Benitez is dead."

"So you think this was a retaliation killing?" Captain Ross asked.

"That I'm not sure of. This one looks professional. From what I saw on last night's murder, that was too sloppy to be a pro, but the gunman might've wanted things to appear that way. Plus, the person who was killed wasn't a major player. This is Jose Benitez; that's a big difference. I doubt they're related but if they are, I'll find out soon enough."

"We need to wrap this up quickly. The minute Omar Benitez finds out that his nephew was killed, he's going to tear my city apart, looking for whoever did it with revenge on his mind."

"I know; we're on it, Captain. Also, we might have a possible witness to the murder."

"What do you mean, might have?"

"Well, someone witnessed it; that's for sure. But, as of right now, we aren't sure they're still alive, who they are, or where they are. I have officers searching behind the shopping mall for a body or any signs of blood. If not, then they're still alive. Also, I have Lewis pulling up the bus schedules for the X2 and the drivers. There were fresh footprints by the bus stop and the shell casings show the killer was aiming in that direction. It seems like the witness was waiting for the bus, so my guess is that he's a local."

"Good job!"

"There's only one problem. If he is still alive, the gunman knows and is looking for him, too," Detective Peterson said.

"That means Omar will be searching for him, trying to get information out of him. Once he gets what he needs, he won't leave him around to tell us anything about it. We need to find that witness!"

"We will, Captain. We will."

"I want you to find the lead detectives on the carryout murder last night. My guess is, if you solve that case, it'll give you more information on this one. If we can bring down the Eastside Riderz and Trinidad and Montello Avenue Crew because of these two murders, that'll be huge. I mean, career-making huge for both of us."

"Captain, you can't be serious. Trinidad and Montello, I can see, but Omar Benitez? DEA and Major Crimes have both been after Benitez for years and haven't gotten anything on him that'll stick. He has more legitimate businesses in this city than he does illegal. The Feds couldn't even build a solid RICO case against him, but I'm supposed to bring him and his organization down over a murder of a small-time dealer at the carryout?"

"Anger has a way of changing things. It clouds the judgment. When anger comes into play, we aren't always as careful as we'd be if we weren't angry. This is his nephew we're talking about. He isn't going to have some low-level soldier take care of it. He's going to want to handle it personally. He won't be hiding in the shadows on this one; mark my words. As a matter of fact, I want you to go break the news to Mr. Benitez yourself and see how he reacts."

"Why?"

"He's the next of kin and you're the investigating detective. He needs to be notified. Also, you can observe his body language. If he looks genuinely surprised, then he didn't know and word hasn't gotten back to him yet. If he's playing things cool, then he knows."

"What about the witness? Time is limited and at a premium right now."

"I agree but, for all we know, the witness is already dead. Omar could've gotten to him, or the assailant. Right now, we have one big puzzle, a lot of pieces, and none in place. Start with Benitez, see how much he knows, and we'll go from there," Captain Ross replied.

"And if Benitez knows nothing?"

"Then we might have a chance. If Benitez doesn't know, once you break the news to him, word will spread like wildfire and it won't take long for him to find out all that we know. Try to keep a closed lid on things. Everyone says you're the best; prove it. Here's your time to shine; bring this one home before we have a serious drug war on our hands that this city doesn't need."

"Gee, thanks a lot, Captain," Detective Peterson stated sarcastically.

"Hey, that's why you get paid the big bucks. Let's do it."

"No problem, Captain. I'm on it."

3

Tony stood outside in the parking lot, waiting on word about the hit. Carlos had talked him into everything. He wasn't content with being a small-time player in the drug game and the only way they could ever achieve any success was with Eastside becoming a distant memory. Many had tried before him; yet, Omar and his crew were still standing tall and even more powerful now than before. Killing Jose was the perfect step to get Omar's attention and have the streets buzzing. If the move was played wrong though, it was also the same risk that would have him and Carlos six feet under.

The building door flung open and Carlos walked outside toward Tony.

"Any word yet?" Carlos asked.

"Yeah, our guy should be here any minute. He said it's done, though," Tony replied.

"Good; that's what I wanted to hear." Carlos had a look of satisfaction on his face. "I wish that I could see the look on Omar's face when he finds out someone touched his ass."

"Yeah, you say that now, but I'm still not sure that was the right move to make. We're talking about Jose; that's definitely going to hit close to home with Omar and you know it."

"That's exactly what we wanted it to do! If you want to be taken serious, you need to do something extreme out here. Hitting

Jose was the perfect power move. We need to let it be known that anyone out here can be touched; even the Eastside Riderz. They aren't untouchable. Omar isn't untouchable. With us getting Jose, he'll see that."

"You've been on an Omar rampage lately. If this is something personal, you need to spill it. That personal shit causes problems. You out here, all hostile and shit. Is there something I need to know?" Tony asked.

"No, I'm cool! It's about to be our time. How can't I get hyped over that?"

"Yeah, I feel you, but we played the first move. Now we have to make sure we're the only ones making the moves or we don't stand a chance. Omar has too much juice for us to go at him straight-up. We gotta be smart about everything so I need you focused. Jose is over and done with; now we need to go to the next move."

"Okay, then say that and stop giving this nigga so much respect. You're acting like we're supposed to lie down for this nigga or something, and that ain't me. Fuck that, I don't think so! He bleeds like I bleed."

"There you go with that shit; always bringing that ego shit into business. Nigga, we didn't take out some ordinary nigga. No, we took out his fucking nephew. Remember, the same nephew that you stressed we had to hit instead of someone else to send the message. Now, you want to be careless about the shit. Well, I'm not. You couldn't even tell me why it had to be Jose."

"Don't worry about all that. Shit! Jose doesn't get a pass because of who he's related to. He's related to the game, and in my eyes; that makes him fair game to me. Anyone in this game can be gotten." Carlos paused. "Did you forget about Moe? It's not like any of them niggas are stressing over killing him last night.

They didn't give a shit about him, so why should we give a shit about Jose?"

Tony looked at Carlos like he was out of his mind for saying that. Moe was a low-level street runner who loved to run his mouth. You didn't have to be there to witness Moe's murder to know exactly what got him killed. It was his mouth and that alone. Even if by chance that wasn't the case, he was far from a vital person within their organization. They could easily find any-one to replace Moe. The only one who would miss him would be his immediate family.

"First of all, you and I both know how Moe was with his mouth. No one really even knows what the hell happened at the carryout yet. Shit, we don't even know, nor do we give a shit. It wasn't business-related. It dealt with him flapping his gums. Plus, this is me you're talking to. Keep that in mind. I know the deal. The hit on Jose was planned long before Moe was killed. It's just coinci-dental that Moe got killed last night."

"That's beside the point."

"Then what is the point, Carlos? Please let my ass know; right now, you aren't saying much about nothing."

"You know what; fuck it. Since I'm not saying nothing, then forget the whole conversation. When's your man going to get here?" Carlos was frustrated.

"Now you want to get off on some bitch shit. Don't start biting your words. You already know I got your back, regardless, and I'm far from going to cry over spilt milk. What's already done is done. Jose is gone and he ain't coming back. That's already been established. My thing is, you have us about to go to war with Omar and the Eastside Riderz. At the very least, I deserve to know why. I'm owed at least that much; the more you talk, the more I get the impression this shit is personal and not business with you."

Carlos glared at Tony. "I put that on everything; this had nothing personal in it. Everything was strictly business; no more or
less. That's why I was cool with how we mapped Jose's murder
out and hired your man to do the contract killing. That way
nothing points at us until we want it to point at us."

"And even with that, we still can't relax like everything is kosher.
Omar's been out in these streets since we were in diapers. You
don't lock a city down or have his type of longevity without
learning how to find out shit you aren't supposed to know, or
others don't want found out. There are no guarantees or safe
bets in this game. We can't relax; we have to stay on point, no
matter what."

Right as Carlos was about to reply, the gate to the courtyard
opened. Both of them turned around to see who it was.

"How did everything go?" Carlos eagerly asked the approaching man.

"Jose was there, like you said. I caught him coming out of the
spot like clockwork and followed him to a more secluded spot.
He didn't even know what hit him," the assassin replied.

"That's what's up!"

"If everything was smooth, then what was so urgent that you
had to come over? I thought we said we'd meet up tomorrow at
the spot for your payment?" Tony said.

"I said, hitting his head went smooth. I didn't say *everything*
went smooth. We've got a small problem on our hands. I was so
concentrated on Jose, I didn't even notice this nigga standing
across the street at the bus stop."

"What are you trying to say? Jose is still alive?"

"Nigga, are you listening? I said, everything went smooth with
me hitting that nigga. He's long gone."

"Then what's the issue? I'm not understanding because if Jose is gone, that means the job has no issues and no problems," Tony replied.

"The issue was the man who witnessed everything. He got away," the hitman replied.

"Who?" Carlos yelled.

"The fucking witness, that's who. He got away."

"So how the fuck is that our problem? He saw your ass and if you were dumb enough to let him get away alive, then that's your problem," Carlos replied.

The hitman approached Carlos. "Don't forget who you're talking to, you little shit! I know everything! Do you really want to play this little game with me? If so, we can play this entire thing out and see how you fair in it. I promise your ass one thing, you won't even come close to winning."

"Nigga, you so dirty right now, neither will you. You adding my name only does what? I can do the years, can you?" Carlos asked.

The hitman smirked. "The years, huh? I'm not even talking about the police. If there's one thing I know, it's that information sells in this town. At this point, I have plenty of information to sell. How do you think you'll fair once Omar finds out who put the hit out on Jose?"

Tony jumped in between the two of them. There was nothing to gain with the witness alive and a lot that could be lost. No one benefited from the situation. "Both of y'all need to calm the fuck down. Look, Carlos didn't mean it like that and you know it."

Not wanting to back down, Carlos shot a look at Tony. Tony gave him a stern look right back.

Tony continued, "So he got away; what's the next move?"

"My assumption is, right now, the police don't know too much of nothing. I haven't really heard anything popping on the streets, but it won't be long before they're looking for the witness."

"How the fuck would they even know there's a witness unless he comes forward?" Carlos looked at Tony. "Yo, your boy is holding out! There's something he isn't telling us."

"Nigga, how fucking stupid are you? You think I peeped the witness and didn't try to kill his ass? No, the minute I saw him, I let loose. The shell casings will give me away. Any rookie cop could look at that shit and tell that I was trying to shoot someone else and being as though there was only one body lying out there, I'm sure they'll be able to put two and two together."

Carlos had no smart remarks.

"Damn, so that means it won't be long before Omar knows there's a witness to everything also," Tony said.

"Exactly," the hitman replied.

Not wanting to seem slower than the others, Carlos didn't say anything, but his facial expression gave away that he was lost.

"I keep telling you, Omar didn't get to be where he is without having some power. He has judges, lawyers, detectives, Feds and more on his payroll. Once word spreads around it was Jose and there's a witness, everything will get back to Omar from his informants," Tony said.

"So what, if Omar finds out? I'm not about to tuck my dick between my legs and hide. I'm not scared of that nigga. If he wants to bring it, then I'm going to bring it right back at him. I fear no fucking man! Fuck Omar!"

The assassin smirked. "Man, you really need to get your boy! Ain't no 'fuck Omar.' Right now he doesn't know shit and that's how we need to keep it. We want him knowing as little as possible."

"Carlos, we already talked about this. You even said it yourself; this has to stay quiet if we're trying to make this move. He's right. The less Omar knows the better."

Carlos rolled his eyes. "Yeah, aiight, but you already said it won't be long before he catches wind that there's a witness."

"Right, but that only gives him a person who *might* be able to give him some pieces of the puzzle but nowhere near everything he needs. See, right now, he doesn't know who hit Jose, or even why. He doesn't realize that he's at war and the true person of interest. It's like the D.C. Sniper. Remember, he was plucking off people at random so once he went after his ex-wife, it would seem random, as if it wasn't him. We want to do the same."

"If we plucking off niggas in his crew, it's not going to take a rocket scientist to figure out that he's at war."

"True; that's why we need to hit key people and not random niggas. One hard strike; by the time we make the second hit, we go straight to Omar and take him out. Boom-boom and done. That way he doesn't have time to go into hiding or plan a counter measure," Tony replied.

"So what now? We find this witness and shut his ass up before the cops and Omar get anything out of him?" Carlos asked.

The hitman grinned. "There you go. Please believe, Omar will get to him long before any cop does. That much we know."

Carlos eyed the assassin suspiciously. "What's in it for you? I mean, besides the fact that you don't want your identity revealed to avoid jail and all?"

"I'm not tripping off that; really. If my identity comes out, cool. Just like you, I can do the years. I have no record and killed a known drug dealer. Any decent lawyer can keep me away from life, off that fact alone. And when I get out, I've proven that I have a skill set that's always going to be needed. But all that depends on if I even make it out alive. I have the same problem you have; Omar."

"Well, that's a given, but you have another angle behind all of this; that's what I'm trying to figure out. What is your angle?"

"It's simple. Money, what else? With Omar out of the picture, that's more work for me. Omar already has his choice of hitters; mostly in-house. As your organization grows, so does my business."

Carlos frowned. "Who said we'd want to continue to do business with you? We can always find others. Shit, with Omar gone, we can probably get his police connects, too."

"Is that right? This I'd love to hear. How? Please, tell me. Shit, can you even tell me who he even has on the inside, or how high up they are?"

Carlos didn't reply.

"You didn't even know Omar was that juiced until your boy just told you not too long ago. I'm all the Intel you have out here in these streets and you know it. And it's like I said, information sells in this town."

"Are you two going to go back and forth all fucking day with this shit?" Tony finally chimed back in. "Damn! This really isn't getting us anywhere. You know where you stand with us and Carlos," he said to the hitman and then turned to Carlos. "And you know damn well we need him, and will continue to use him, so go ahead with that bullshit." Tony looked at both of them and there were no objections. "Thank you! Where do we go from here with the witness so we can shut him up?"

"I don't know yet. He was waiting for the bus so he must live in that area. I'll put my ear to the ground and see what comes up. I need to find out exactly what the police know and if he's been running his mouth already to anyone in the neighborhood. It won't be long before he starts. Seeing what he saw, he has to tell someone. That isn't info that you can sit on like nothing happened. Once he does that, we'll find him."

"Then that sounds like the plan. Once you eliminate the witness, we'll finish off Omar's organization," Tony said.

"That's cool," the hitman replied.

Tony turned toward Carlos. Carlos didn't say anything.

"Are you good?" Tony asked. Carlos moved like he was going to turn away. Tony quickly grabbed him. "Slim, are you good?"

"Yeah, nigga, I'm cool," Carlos shot back.

The hitman was irritated. "Look here, if your boy isn't on board, it's cool. I can find the witness, take care of that, and cut my losses. Y'all can handle Omar and go at his folks on your own. It doesn't make me no never mind, for real."

"It's not that serious. He's cool. There's nothing to worry about. I have everything under control. Handle the witness and we'll meet up on the rest." The hitman looked at Tony. "Seriously, go ahead," Tony said, trying to reassure him.

"Yeah, aiight," the hitman said and then left.

Tony waited until the coast was clear, until he was alone with Carlos.

"What's up with the bitch tactics? Seriously, like you really were acting like a little girl or something."

"Whatever!"

"See that's what I'm talking about. You're the one who wanted to make a power move on Eastside and I backed everything, blind. I've been there with you all the way, one hundred."

"What's your point? I know all of that!" Carlos shot back.

"You and your fucking attitude are my point. This is business, and whenever you get your feelings and shit involved, that's when you start to get careless. You aren't thinking and you're acting off impulse. Right now, every move you want to make, or every reply you're giving, is off impulse. I need you to get out of your feelings and remember: this is business."

"I hear you, but I don't trust that nigga. I'm sorry, I just don't. It's like he has all the answers for everything. I don't like that. You can't trust a nigga like that."

"Fine, but he has a job to do and we started this thing with a plan. Let him do his job; we carry out our plans and then we can go our separate ways, if that's what we decide to do. But right now, I need you focused on our plan and not him. I need my man's eyes back on the prize. You hear me?" Tony pleaded.

"Yeah, I hear you."

"Aiight, that's my man right there. Now, are you going to tell me, why Jose?"

Carlos started laughing. "There you go with that again? How you get back on that?"

"You still aren't going to clue me in? Really, that's how you're going to do me?"

"Just drop it. We sent the message. It's open season on the Benitez clan and them Eastside bitches. Just let that ride," Carlos replied.

"Man, I swear, I need a drink, messing around with you."

4

D etective Peterson realized that his captain was right. Omar was the center of everything. He needed to find out how much Omar knew and then he could map out a better game plan on how to proceed with his investigation. Time was of the essence and when you have no clue how much time you're working with, that's the first thing that needs to be figured out. For years, the Metropolitan Police Department knew it had leaks to Benitez but how many and who had never been detected. No one even knew what precinct the possible leaks were in.

Though he needed to handle as much as possible, if not everything, by himself, Detective Peterson wasn't dumb enough to go around Congress Heights in Southeast D.C. alone. It didn't matter how confident he was that he'd be safe. He wasn't about to take the chance of finding out what the consequences would be if he were wrong. Before heading over to Congress Heights, he called Inspector Lewis and told him to meet him there.

As Detective Peterson pulled up to the apartment complex on Thirteenth Street, he noticed Lewis's car already parked. He parked right behind it. Lewis got out of the car as Detective Peterson pulled up.

"What's the plan?" Lewis asked as he approached the car.

"Nothing much; we're just about to shake things up a little bit."

"How? Did you find out anything new?"

"Just watch and listen; that's all I need you to do right now."

They approached the courtyard where everyone was congregated.

Omar and his crew were sitting in lawn chairs out front. They'd spotted Peterson and Lewis the minute they pulled up so all possible illegal activity had ceased.

"Good afternoon, detectives. How can we help you?" Omar asked as they approached.

"Omar Benitez?" Detective Peterson asked.

"That would be me." Omar stood up and courteously extended his hand. Detective Peterson ignored his gesture and didn't shake his hand. Omar smiled. "How can I help you this morning, gentlemen?"

"Actually, you can't help us today. We're here to notify you about the death of your nephew, Jose. He was gunned down earlier this morning."

Everyone looked around at each other; lost. The news obviously had everyone shook up, none more than Omar himself. The smile that was visibly painted over his face evaporated.

"I'm sorry but you must have my Jose confused with someone else. Especially not no murder; no one would touch my nephew," Omar responded.

It was obvious he had no idea what had happened. The news hadn't reached him yet. He was in denial and didn't want to believe that his nephew had been murdered.

Detective Peterson approached Omar and took out a picture of Jose's lifeless body lying on the pavement and showed it to him.

"Unfortunately, there's no mistake. Your nephew *is* the one who was killed earlier this morning."

Omar didn't want to even look at the picture. He was still in denial. It had to have been a mistake; someone who resembled Jose. He turned and looked at his lieutenant.

"Call Jose's cell and get my nephew on the phone so this detective can get out of here with this nonsense."

"Be my guest, but I promise you that Jose won't answer the phone," Detective Peterson replied sarcastically.

Omar stared at Lewis as if he was attempting to intimidate him. Omar's lieutenant was a nervous wreck after each passing ring of the phone. He didn't want to be the one to confirm the obvious. As Detective Peterson had predicted, there was no answer. The phone went to Jose's voicemail.

Detective Peterson had to have been telling the truth. Jose was indeed dead. He looked at Omar as he hung up the phone and shook his head, signaling there was no answer. Omar had been around long enough to know never to show his true emotions. He could feel them starting to get the best of him. He quickly caught himself before he responded.

"What happened to my nephew, detective?"

"As I stated, he was gunned down this morning."

"That part we've established but what exactly happened? Where did this happen?'

"At the corner of Minnesota Avenue and Benning Road," Lewis responded.

Detective Peterson looked at Lewis, upset. It was clear he wanted to tell Omar about his nephew's death without giving him any specific details about the investigation. Lewis could tell by Detective Peterson's expression that he had messed up and looked away. Once Lewis said where the murder had taken place, a light bulb went off in Omar's head.

"Do you have any suspects in custody, detective?" Omar asked.

"Mr. Benitez, we're actively working your nephew's murder and will bring his assailant to justice."

Omar recognized that that meant they didn't. He waved for his lieutenant to come to him and whispered something into his ear.

Once he was finished, his lieutenant took out his cell phone and went into the apartment building.

Omar continued, "Please don't get offended or take it personal if I don't believe you, detective. I know how you people feel about me and it's obviously clear, by the tone of your voice, how you personally feel regarding myself and the situation. I get the sense that you're getting some type of satisfaction out of my pain, and my nephew's death."

"Mr. Benitez, I take pride in being a very upfront and honest person. As a man, I can stand before you and tell you face-to-face that I don't give a shit about you, or your nephew. There's not a doubt or question about it. However, what I do care about is my job and honoring the badge that I wear. With that comes getting justice for every one of my victims. It doesn't matter who they are. I don't get to choose my victims. And the minute your nephew became one of them, he started receiving the same treatment: justice."

"I can respect that, detective."

"Good, I'm glad we have an understanding. But I also want you to understand that this is my investigation. I know you just told your little goon to do something. So before you start to try to play police and get street justice, I want you and all these little idiots out here to hear me and hear me good. Stay out of my investigation! If I find out you're involved in any way, please believe, I'll bring your asses down." Omar didn't respond. Detective Peterson began to get frustrated. "Is there something you want to tell me that'll help my investigation? You can start with, why your nephew was over in that area? Who would he have been with?"

"I have no idea. Aside from what you might've heard about me or what you might think, I'm a respectable businessman within this community. My associate merely went inside to break the news to the rest of my family and, of course, my nephew's mother. She has the right to know that her only son has been murdered. Don't you think so, detective?"

"Yeah, okay, I've said what I needed to say. If you choose not to listen to my warning, that's up to you, but I surely promise you that if I see one drop of blood on these streets behind your nephew being killed, I'll be a man of my word and come back here," Detective Peterson reassured Omar.

"Detective, I'm a simple man who enjoys simple things. Your threats far from scare me. My nephew was loved by many people. I can't control the actions of others or what happens in these streets. I'm only but one man. D.C. isn't called the 'murder capital' for no reason. Look at what happened to my poor nephew. Things happen out here. You surely can't blame me for every little thing that happens. But if you feel the need to, that's fine. I can't control that either."

Detective Peterson cracked a smile. "Very cute!" He moved in closer to Omar. "Test me if you want to and I promise, I'll nail your ass to the wall."

"Is that yet another threat, detective?"

"No, far from it, Mr. Benitez."

"I will say this though, detective. You're more than welcome to get in line. Right now, you have the FBI, DEA, and a lot of your other fellow officers in front of you who've been trying to... How did you put it? Ah yes, nail my ass to the wall for years." Omar started laughing.

"That might be true, but I'm not them. The difference between me and the rest of them is that I don't fear you. You don't scare me. Plus, it's like you said. This is D.C. and things happen out here in these streets. If you feel the need, test my reach."

"Well then, detective, let the games begin. Is there anything else?"

"No, that's all. You enjoy the rest of your day and please give my condolences to your sister for the loss of her child," Detective Peterson replied.

"I most certainly shall and I'm sure she'll appreciate that. But if you really want to show your condolences, bring her son's killer to justice."

Omar turned and headed toward the apartment complex directly behind him. Detective Peterson and Lewis both headed to their cars.

"Do you think that was smart?" Lewis asked.

"What?"

"Antagonizing him; shit no. Pissing him off?"

"He's a man, just like I am. He puts his pants on one leg at a time, just like I do. He might control a good part of D.C. but I wanted to make it perfectly clear, I'm not a part of the D.C. he does control."

"Okay, but pissing him off does what? What possible good does it do, except adding your name to his list of enemies?"

"What good does giving him information regarding my murder investigation do either? What were you thinking, telling him anything? Your job wasn't to speak. The only thing I needed you to do was stand there and act like a damn cop. Nothing more and nothing less."

"I apologize. Maybe I shouldn't have said anything. I didn't think telling him where Jose was killed would hurt anything."

"Well, you were wrong. Not only did it point him in the right direction, but it unlocked a clue. Remember, we know nothing. We only know that Jose was killed. We don't know why or what he was doing over there but it was obvious that Omar does. It won't be long before he has more pieces to this puzzle than we do."

"I'm sorry. It's not like he wasn't going to find out. Shit, he probably was pulling your leg and already knew."

"He didn't know anything; that much I could see. None of them knew, for that matter, but what you said hit a nerve. Soon they'll know a lot more, if not everything. Where are we with the Metrobus drivers?"

"Last I heard, all of them had been contacted and were on their way to the station right now."

"I'm going to head on over there. I want you to stay here and keep an eye on Omar's crew. Whatever Omar is up to, he'll have his lieutenant out and about. I want you to follow him until I get someone else to tail him. Do not tell anyone anything. If you find out anything, you call me and me only. I need to keep a tight lid on this investigation," Detective Peterson said.

"Do you really think all that is necessary?"

Detective Peterson looked at Lewis, wondering why he was questioning every order and being difficult. It was unlike Lewis.

Lewis continued, "All I'm saying is, do you really think Omar would be that careless after what you just said to him?"

Detective Peterson got into his car and turned on the ignition.

"Maybe he will and maybe he won't; that I don't know. But what I do know is that I don't want to take the chance that he won't and he actually does."

Lewis sighed. "Okay, no problem."

Detective Peterson drove away. Lewis started to walk to his car to get in it and wait. He spotted Peterson turn down a side street and waited until he was no longer within eyesight and stopped. He turned around and made his way back toward the apartment complex. Someone from Omar's crew stopped him as he reached the courtyard. Lewis stared at him like the guy had lost his mind.

The crew member stepped aside so Lewis could enter the building.

Omar was standing at the base of the steps, talking to his lieutenant. Both of them turned to Lewis once he entered and approached him. Before Lewis knew it, Omar had taken out a pistol from his waistline and had it to his head while he had him choked up against the wall.

"My nephew was killed hours ago and I'm just hearing this now!"

"I swear, I couldn't get word to you any sooner without bringing suspicion to myself."

"I don't give a shit; this was my NEPHEW!" Omar yelled.

"I understand and I know. I promise you, I didn't have a chance to call or nothing."

Omar's lieutenant patted him on his shoulder. Omar let go of Lewis and gave the gun to his lieutenant.

"What happened?"

"We really have no clue. Whoever it was, he's a professional. Peterson thinks it might be retaliation by someone from the Trinidad and Montello Avenue Crew."

"Retaliation? For what?" Omar questioned.

"One of their members was killed last night," Lewis replied.

"Tito, what is he talking about?" Omar asked his lieutenant.

"Some kid was popped at the carryout, but we had nothing to do with it. It wasn't official business. From what I know, he was going off at the mouth and Manuel closed it," Tito replied.

"So pretty much, you're telling me that the police have nothing? There's no way any of them would bring my nephew into this over that. Plus, they're incapable of even knowing where Jose would be this morning. Their arms don't reach that high."

"Well, someone witnessed it. That much the police do know. Whoever he is, he got away. We didn't find a body and, right now, there have been no suspicious missing person reports."

"Are you sure someone witnessed it?" Omar asked.

"We're positive. That's what Peterson is working on right now, identifying the witness."

"Okay, well, as I'm sure you know, we need to find his ass first. The minute you know or hear anything, make sure that I'm made aware of it. My patience is very thin, so please don't make the same mistake twice."

"That's no problem. I definitely won't make the same mistake again," Lewis replied.

Omar looked at the door, giving Lewis the hint that his presence was no longer wanted, or needed. Lewis headed for the door and left the building.

"Correct me if I'm wrong, Tito. You don't think it's possible Trinidad and Montello Avenue is behind this, do you?"

"No, I don't. One, it was Manuel who killed their friend, so why not go after him? It's not like he's hard to reach. If anyone really wanted to get him, he could be found easily. Two, this is Jose we're talking about and if he was over on Benning and Minnesota, that means he was making a drop. Who within their crew would know that type of information? I could see if he was close to their neighborhood. Then again, maybe it could've been a wrong place, wrong time kind of situation. But it wasn't. He was leaving a stash house. I definitely don't think it was them."

Omar thought over everything Tito had said. It all made sense but he still was unsure. "I was thinking the same thing, but what if we're wrong? That's what troubles me. None of this is making any sense and I don't like it when I'm in the dark. Make sure our people are on high alert until we have more answers. I don't want to take any chances; whoever got to Jose knows more about us than I'm comfortable with."

"Okay," Tito replied.

"Also, get over to Maria's and find out what she knows. See if Jose ever made it to her place before he was killed and finished the drop, or if our product was taken as well. I want you to handle this personally."

"Okay, boss, but what about that detective, Peterson, or Lewis?"

"Lewis is dead to us at this point. Once he finds out where the witness is, we'll cut our ties with him. I'm not buying this he couldn't reach out to us bullshit. In my eyes, he's shown his true colors, and worth. He can save that mistake shit for someone else. Mistake, my ass! But this Peterson fellow definitely does worry me a bit. We need to put someone within the department on him; to at least slow him down. I have a feeling he might prove to be a thorn in my side and those don't kill you, but are always a pain in the ass."

Tito started laughing. "The smart ones always prove to be."

"Right, it's something about him. The look in his eyes said a lot. He had determination in them. Yeah, we must keep an eye on him and be very careful."

5

Derrick rode the V8 Metrobus all the way to the Archives Navy Memorial Subway station at Seventh Street and Constitution Avenue in Northwest Washington, D.C. His mind was racing a hundred miles a minute. He was in a serious jam and didn't know what to do. He wasn't sure if he should report what he had seen to the police. He wasn't the most street savvy but realized that witnesses never fared well. Most disappeared before the trial ever began. But he needed the police if the killer was to ever be caught.

What if the police thought he was the actual killer or involved in the murder some way? It wasn't like Derrick had stuck around to wait for the police, so he wasn't sure if they would try to use that against him. It wasn't like he had really thought things through as he was being targeted. It was hard to weigh those options when bullets were dashing past his head.

Derrick had a bunch of questions but no answers. Even though he didn't know what to do, he figured one person definitely would. He took out his cell phone and called Thomas.

"Hello," Thomas answered the phone groggily.

"Thomas."

"Damn, you just don't want me to get any sleep, do you?"

"What are you even still doing asleep? You should've been up by now. Never mind that; that's beside the point. I really need your help right now."

"I'm up; what's going on? Please don't tell me you got to work late and got fired?"

"Fuck work right now! I have more serious problems."

"Damn, problems must be contagious around here these days. I haven't been able to get an ounce of sleep this morning because of all the sirens racing up and down the street. I even had to call my editor and tell him that I'd be a late so I could try to get some sleep."

"What! Did the police knock on our door?" Derrick asked.

"No, why would they knock on our door? They're up the street. After I noticed the constant noise, I went outside to see what the hell was going on. Man, I found out Jose Benitez was killed so it's hectic over here right about now."

"Who?"

"Jose Benitez; he runs with the Eastside Riderz. Actually, I shouldn't say run with; he's a major player. Anyway, he was shot at the corner of—"

Derrick cut him off. "Let me guess, the corner of Minnesota and Benning?"

"Yeah, how did you know?" Thomas asked.

"One, because you said the police are up the street and two, because I saw the whole damn thing this morning. The shit happened right in front of me. That's why I'm calling you."

"Please tell me that you're kidding," Thomas replied.

"I was almost killed! Does it sound like I'm playing any damn games?" Derrick shot back at him.

"Okay, calm down; I got it. You aren't playing. My bad! Damn, I wish you were playing, though; this is more than serious. This is life-threatening."

"I could've sworn I just said that I was almost killed earlier this morning. I'm pretty sure I got the message that this is a life-threatening situation since my life has already been threatened."

"Okay, aiight, just tell me what happened!"

"All I know is, while I was at the bus stop, some guy came up behind whoever this Jose person was and shot him. Once he dropped him, he shot him again, twice in the head. He was so focused on Jose, he didn't even notice I was out there. Afterwards, he surveyed the area and that's when he saw me. The minute he spotted me, he started shooting at me."

"You aren't hurt or anything, are you?"

"Naw, I'm a little shook up by everything, but physically, I'm fine. I ran behind the shopping mall, lost him, and then I jumped on the V8. There was so much traffic and then the bus broke down and we had to get on another bus. I'm just getting downtown."

"Is that where you are now?"

"Yeah, I was just trying to get away; I didn't really care where I went. Now I'm trying to figure out what steps to take next. I don't know what to do. I mean, I need to go to the police but—"

"That's the last thing you need to do, or place you want to go," Thomas said as he cut him off.

"Huh, why? The police need to know what happened so they can catch this guy. I'm sure he's going to be looking for me to finish off the job so he doesn't go to jail. I might not know much but I do know that people like that don't like to have witnesses who can testify about them committing crimes."

"True but if you go to the police, you'll be dead before Monday. That much I can pretty much assure you," Thomas replied.

"How? You would think that would make things better. If I tell the police everything, wouldn't they want to protect me?"

"Damn, you really are green, aren't you? You don't know anything 'bout the Eastside Riderz, do you?"

"No, not really. Why should I?"

"Sometimes I wonder if we grew up in the same neighborhood or if you just used to visit around there or something. Does the name Omar Benitez mean anything?"

"Yeah, I know who that is. He's that big-time drug dealer that never goes to jail. He's always getting off."

"Okay, well, Jose Benitez was Omar Benitez's nephew. Omar Benitez is the head of the Eastside Riderz and pretty much runs most of D.C. He probably has half of the police department working for him. That's how he always avoids jail; either he's tipped off before the police move in, or he buys his freedom. If he finds out you saw what happened to Jose, he's probably going to think you had something to do with it."

"So what should I do?" Derrick asked, on the verge of a panic attack. He tried to calm himself while Thomas was thinking. "Maybe if I go to Omar, he won't think anything. I'm sure he'd want to know who killed his nephew. Wouldn't that help? That way, I came to him first and never went to the cops."

"And what are you going to tell him? It's not like you know any of the players in the city so I'm sure you don't know who killed Jose."

"I don't know his name but I can at least describe him."

"And how do you even get to Omar? You aren't connected enough to set up a meeting with him directly, so whoever you speak to is going to take the info you give them and relate it to Omar. But let's say, by chance, they allow you to speak to him. The minute you tell him whatever information he needs, which isn't much, he no longer needs you," Thomas said.

"Okay and? Isn't that a good thing?" Derrick was confused.

"Meaning he won't need you alive anymore, you idiot. It's no different than the killer trying to get at you. Why would Omar leave a potential witness alive to testify against him after he avenges his nephew's murder?"

"This is different than the killer. I physically saw him kill Jose. I wouldn't be there to see Omar avenge Jose's murder. Plus, why would he even think I'd testify against him? I went to him, instead of the police with the information. That should be my proof right there. If anything, I would think he would be grateful."

"Let me give you a quick lesson about the streets. One, you never leave a potential witness alive who could testify against you. It doesn't matter what the situation is. Two, he doesn't know you. You're coming to him out of the blue, saying you have information about his nephew. You don't think the cops realize who Jose Benitez is. I'm sure they've already spoken to Omar. Now here you come with so-called information; he's liable to think you're working with or for the cops. He isn't going to take the chance to trust you."

"Well, shit, I don't know! I'm trying to think of something. It's not like I know what to do. If I did, then I would've done it and wouldn't be on the phone with you. You sitting here saying that I can't go to the police and going to Omar wouldn't do any good, so what then? What the hell should I do?"

"Your best bet is to lay low right now. Talk to no one. I mean, no one. Don't tell a soul what you saw. To be on the safe side, I wouldn't even come back to the crib for a while. At least, not until all this has blown over," Thomas suggested.

"I can do that. I'll go chill at my mother's."

"No, that's too close to home. You need to start thinking like the cops, Omar, and the killer know everything about you. That means the apartment and your mom's house are the first places they'll look for you. Right now, your mother is safer with you nowhere near her."

"So where the hell am I supposed to go then?" Derrick questioned.

"I don't know. You don't have anywhere else you could go and lay low for a while? My thinking is if the police catch the killer, then you should be good. Omar wouldn't have any use for you; he'll know the police have him. And the police won't have any use for you; they would've had some type of evidence to lead them to the killer, and he won't be able to get to you because he'll be in jail."

"All of that sounds good but I've yet to hear where it is I should be going since I don't have anywhere else to stay."

Thomas ignored Derrick's question. "Did anyone else see you? Was anyone else out there?"

"Huh, no, not that I saw. It was just me and the man who was trying to kill me. I didn't really have time to take a survey to see if anyone else was there during all of that."

"Point taken. So with no one else out there, that means only the killer is looking for you right now?"

"Wow, say it like there's nothing to worry about, why don't you? I mean, I can only identify him in a lineup or whatever."

"True but you also have to keep in mind that he killed Jose Benitez so the police are far from his main concern right now, if he realizes who he shot. He's more concerned about Omar catching up to him."

"Either way, finding me more than likely is his number one priority."

"Yeah, you're right. You lay low and I'm going to head in to work and see what's flying around the newsroom."

"You're a sports reporter. What can you possibly find out?"

"How I find shit out is none of your business. Regardless of what you think, I'm a reporter. It doesn't matter what type. I need you to lay low until I find out exactly what's going on with the situation. I'll know exactly how serious shit really is and we can go from there."

"Again, I ask you, where the hell am I supposed to stay and *lay low* while you're doing all of this? You still haven't told me that part yet."

"You're going to have to find something to do for right now. I need some time, Derrick; shit! I'm pretty sure you can crash at Lisa's for a few days but I need some time to talk to her and make up an excuse. That'll buy us at least a little bit of time and then, if we need to find a place more permanent for you, we'll do that."

"I don't know about that," Derrick replied.

"I said, just for right now. Look, I don't feel comfortable with you shacking up with my damn girl cither, but we need something temporary. It's not like you have a girl, or any damn friends. Shit, I'm pretty much your only damn friend. Actually, I'm your *only* friend. We don't have a lot of options, Derrick. This is going to have to do for now."

"Okay, fine!"

"You said you're at 7th and Constitution, right? Head up to Gallery Place and check out a couple of movies. That should take care of your afternoon right there. We'll meet up at Lucky Strikes bowling alley around four-thirty."

"Cool; thanks, Thomas," Derrick said.

"It's nothing; you be safe and watch your back. Remember, for right now, talk to no one."

"Don't worry; I won't."

6

Detective Peterson walked into the interview room at the 6th District precinct. Three men were inside, waiting patiently at the table.

"Hello, gentlemen. My name's Detective Peterson. I'm sorry to have had you all waiting for so long."

"Don't even worry about it; it's all-good," Bus Driver Three said. "We're all still on the clock. Any paid time away from work is alright by me."

"Yeah, me too. However I'm interested in knowing what this all about," Bus Driver One added.

"There was a murder earlier today at the corner of Minnesota Avenue and Benning Road and I'm hoping that one of you might have some useful information that'll be able to help us out with solving it."

"Yeah, I saw all the commotion this morning when you guys were on the scene. I figured it had to have been something big that happened, but I wouldn't be able to help you out. Your guys were already on the scene by the time I got to that area for my first run," Bus Driver Two replied.

"So were you able to finish your route today?" Detective Peterson asked.

"Yeah, I was able to. Dispatch was already aware of everything and had me rerouted to go around the crime scene."

"Did you have any regulars who normally get on at the Minnesota and Benning stop who didn't get on the bus today?" Detective Peterson asked.

"I had a lot of them who didn't get on because of the detour. Either they didn't know about it, they were too busy out there being nosey, or they walked up to the subway station instead and caught the train. I don't think any of my regular passengers from that stop got on the bus today. You boys had pretty much everything in that area locked down tight and blocked off."

Detective Peterson looked at the other two drivers. "What about either of you?"

Bus Driver Three quickly spoke, "I come through that area after him, so I definitely wouldn't be any help. I had the same luck. My bus was pretty empty for passengers coming from that area. Either people got on my bus before the detour or after." Bus Driver One was steadily trying to think back. Bus Driver Three continued, "Plus, that is a very popular stop."

"What do you mean by that?" Detective Peterson asked.

"It's a major intersection; I have a lot of people who get on at that bus stop. I have everyone from school kids, to working-class citizens, to people needing a ride to their next destination. Even if someone was missing, I doubt that I'd have even noticed, to be honest with you. Around that time, my bus is jam-packed and I have people standing for the remainder of the ride. That doesn't leave much time to associate and make friends or anything with my regulars. Not with that route at that time, at least."

"Okay, well, thank you, gentlemen. It was worth a try. If you can think of anything or something comes to mind, I don't care how small, here's my card. Please don't hesitate to give me a call. You'd be surprised how, sometimes, the smallest of things turn out to be the biggest break in a case."

Detective Peterson handed each of them one of his business cards.

"Hey, I'm sorry we weren't able to be of any help," Bus Driver Two said.

"It's still early so don't worry, you might still be able to help. If someone knows something, people love to gossip and what better way than on the ride to work on the bus in the morning? You never know what you might hear," Detective Peterson said. "You gentlemen have a good day, though."

Each of the drivers exited the room. Detective Peterson grabbed the empty cups that were left on the table and started to throw them in the trash when the door reopened and Bus Driver One walked back into the interview room.

"Detective," he said, getting Detective Peterson's attention.

Detective Peterson turned around and noticed Bus Driver One standing there. "Yes, did you leave something behind?"

"No, it's nothing like that. Is it true that Jose Benitez was the one who was killed?"

Detective Peterson was reluctant to answer but the driver was asking for a specific reason.

"I see the streets really have been talking. Didn't know who was murdered was out there already. Yes, it's true; he's the one who was murdered this morning."

The driver's facial expression said something was on his mind, but because of who was killed, he was reluctant to say anything. It was obvious he was pondering whether to be helpful or keep his information to himself.

Detective Peterson could tell Bus Driver One knew something. "Is there something you know that you aren't saying?"

"I don't know. I'm not trying to get involved. I mean, you're the police and all, but I'm the one who has to live out in these streets. I'm definitely not trying to go up against the Eastside Riderz. I'm a bus driver. I have to drive in that neighborhood every day. You know what I'm saying?"

"I understand. Depending on exactly what you know, I'm sure we can keep your name out of it. No one has to know what you saw or that you told me anything but you and me."

Bus Driver One stood there, debating on whether or not he should say something.

Detective Peterson continued, "Did you see something this morning?"

"No, nothing like that," Bus Driver One quickly responded.

"Well, like I said, whatever you tell me will stay between you and me. I promise you, it won't leave this room."

"I'm not sure how much this'll help you but you asked about regular passengers who weren't on the bus. There's this one guy who I know would've been on the bus this morning and he wasn't. My bus is one of the first ones in that area so it's not as crowded as the other buses. I know my regulars. Anyway, there's one guy who usually gets on the bus at that stop. I even tried to wait a little bit for him. He isn't the best with time so I thought he might've overslept or something. He never showed so I left. I figured maybe he called out sick this morning or something."

"Do you know his name?" Detective Peterson asked.

"All I know is his first name. It's Derrick, but I do know he isn't a street guy. He's that college, preppy type. There's no way I can see how he'd have anything to do with Eastside or anyone out in these streets, for that matter."

"That's even better. Do you know where he lives?"

"No, not his exact address, but he did once tell me that he lives on or off of Minnesota Avenue. I can't say which for sure."

"Okay, well, something is better than nothing," Detective Peterson replied.

"I'm sorry that I couldn't help you out more. Like I said, it might not be anything at all. He could've overslept."

"It doesn't hurt to check it out and make sure. Anything will help right now. You've given me more information than I had five minutes ago." Detective Peterson extended his hand to shake Bus Driver One's hand. "Look, I can't thank you enough for coming back and talking to me. I'm from these same streets so I understand exactly what you're going through. I promise what we talked about stays between us."

"Thanks, I appreciate that. I definitely don't want people to think I know something or I'm talking. I hope you catch the guy." He turned to head out the door and stopped as a thought hit him. "Hold up! He has a roommate. I think his name is Tomas or Tommy. It's something like that. He rode the bus a couple of times with him. I think he's a reporter or something. I'm not too sure but I believe he works for the *Washington Inquirer*."

"Thanks a lot!"

"Not a problem," Bus Driver One said and then left the room.

Detective Peterson hoped that the bus driver's intuition was wrong and Derrick didn't oversleep. Hopefully he was out there right when the murder happened and he was the witness he was searching for.

✠✠✠

Tito walked down the hall to Maria's apartment. He noticed her door was already cracked open. He pulled out his pistol and cautiously entered the apartment. Tito checked every room until he found Maria. She was lying in the half-filled bathroom tub with two bullet wounds in the crown of her forehead.

"Shit!" Tito yelled.

Tito searched the apartment for any possible leads. He tossed it up and down. He checked under the bed and found the missing cocaine still in the drop-off bag. If she had the cocaine, then that meant Jose was able to complete the drop. But, that also meant Jose's murder wasn't the result of a robbery.

Unless Maria was behind the robbery but, even still, why would she be dead and better yet, why would the cocaine still be in her possession? Jose had to have been killed behind something personal. Tito grabbed the cocaine and got out of the apartment. All he needed was for the cops to show up and then he'd have Maria's murder put on his head.

Once Tito was in the car, he called Omar to tell him to meet him at Fort Dupont Park in ten minutes.

Omar didn't hesitate. Whatever Tito had found out, or wanted to discuss, was important. Omar pulled up and got out of the car. Omar and Tito walked into the park so that they could talk freely. This way, if anyone was following them, there was no way they could listen in.

"What did Maria say?"

"She wasn't able to say much of anything. Someone beat me to her. I found her in the tub with two in her head," Tito replied.

"This isn't good."

"I know. I can't make any sense of it. Whoever killed her had to have done so after Jose left. The coca was still there."

"So this wasn't a robbery but a hit!"

"That's how it's looking."

"Where's the coca now?" Omar asked.

"It's in the car."

Omar paused to try to make sense of the situation. "She played some part in his death."

"You think? Then why not kill Jose and her at the same time in the apartment?"

"That would be more typical of a robbery. But for him to kill Jose, then come back and kill Maria, it's obvious he was cleaning up his mess. She had to have known something that would've led us to him. How would she know anything, unless she played a role in it?"

"Well, to be on the safe side, I grabbed her cell phone before I left, to see who she was talking to. There were a few calls to someone named Carlos. But none were made around the time Jose would've been over there or was killed, though. The last time she called him was a couple of days ago."

"So why are you telling me this? We both know Maria liked to fuck. Carlos could've been one of the many men she dealt with," Omar replied.

"This is true. However, once I saw the coca still there, I knew, regardless, whether she was in it or not, Jose's murder was something personal. What I figured was someone Maria was fucking saw Jose leaving out, took him out, and then went back and finished Maria off."

"Maybe, but what does this Carlos fellow have to do with anything? Was he fucking Maria?"

"I'm not sure, but the name caught my attention. Carlos is also the name of one of the young punks from around Trinidad. He and another dude actually run the crew over there. I remembered how the detective said that he thought Jose was murdered in retaliation over the kid Manuel popped the other day."

"And you believe he's capable of this?"

"Capable of murder? Yes, definitely. I don't think he's capable of a pulling off a planned execution, though. Whoever did this planned it all the way through and also knew what lose ends to clean up. This has to be the work of a pro. It was way too clean to be Carlos's handiwork. Also, he would've taken the coca as an extra bonus. A pro has no benefit in taking it; he doesn't move product so it does him no good."

Omar didn't say anything; he continued to walk.

Tito continued, "Omar, you know me. I'm a man of logic; not coincidence. The name could be coincidental, but logic tells me that it's a sign; no coincidence at all. Maybe he had nothing to do with it. Maybe he knows nothing; maybe he does. But what we do know is that Jose's dead and *maybe* won't cut it. We need the answers to *maybe*."

"I agree, my friend. If it was a planned robbery, why leave the coca? If you were smart enough to plan out the hit and carry it out without a single clue, then you know where the coca is and would've taken it as well."

"Maybe it wasn't about the drugs, Omar. Maybe it was to make us believe it was, to take us off the true scent. The killer might've only known that her crib was a drop spot, planned to kill Jose there, and make it seem like it was a robbery. But unless he was fucking Maria, then he'd have no way of knowing about the hidden lock box under the floorboard where the coca was stashed."

"I agree and that's the riddle we need to solve. Did it even look like he searched for it? Was the house tossed?"

"No, everything was in place," Tito responded.

"Maria was a part of it then. That's where we need to start; with her and her associates."

"I don't have Maria selling information on Jose. She's loved him since they were kids."

"Never underestimate anyone, my friend; especially the heart of a scorned woman, or the power of money. Both are unpredictable and capable of the very thing you think they aren't. We both know that Maria definitely played a part in this; that's why she isn't here to tell us about it. She betrayed me and my nephew, so why's it hard to believe that she'd give up information on him?"

"So what do you want to do now? You want me to pay Carlos a visit and handle that situation?" Tito asked.

"No, we need to keep this one close to the vest and play it real smart. Right now, we aren't too sure whether he had anything to do with it and, if he did, we don't know what role he played. He could be another piece to this puzzle, or nothing at all. The phone was left there for someone to find so someone wanted us to know about Carlos. Carlos wouldn't point us at him. Why are we being pointed in his direction? That's the answer we need to find out. Let's go pay him and his associates a visit together and see how they react to things; then we'll go from there."

"What if he doesn't shed any light on the situation? What if he really doesn't know anything at all? It could've been another person with the name Carlos in her phone. We might be on the completely wrong trail."

"This is true, but these are all questions that we need to answer. Whoever Carlos is, he knows something. Whether we have the right Carlos or not, we shall see. If not, I'll put Lewis on finding this person."

"Lewis? He has already proven himself untrustworthy. Why give him such an important assignment?" Tito questioned.

"His mistakes are the very reason why we ask Lewis to find out the information. He already knows he's in the doghouse because of his past mistakes. He doesn't want to be on shaky ground no more than anyone else would, so right now, he'll go all out to prove his worth to us. If we put him on it, he'll go far and beyond to find out the information we need in an attempt to smooth things over with us. Trust me when I tell you, he's the perfect person to put on it if we draw a blank. Remember, regardless of what he does, it won't change how we feel about him, or the consequences he has waiting for him. We're only using him to our benefit now."

Tito liked the plan and started to smile. "Man, I'd hate to get on your bad side."

Omar patted Tito on the shoulder. "My friend, you're the only family I have left. My bad side is something that you never have to worry about."

7

Thomas walked in the newsroom. Everything was a madhouse. He quickly found out that word about Jose Benitez's murder had spread like wildfire. That raised questions of panic, but once he found out there were no leads and no possible witnesses, he felt a little at-ease. If the police knew nothing, Derrick had a better chance. This entire case was a news reporter's nightmare. There were absolutely no leads, cracks, or even a slimmer of any breaks. The usual leaks any good reporter could find were all dry.

Thomas started to think that maybe the situation wasn't as bad as he had initially thought. If the police had no leads or information about the case and the streets knew nothing, then there was nothing that could get reported back to Omar. But that only solved one of their problems. If the police had no leads, that meant they were nowhere near close to catching the killer. With him still out on the loose, finding Derrick had to be his number one priority.

Thomas picked up the phone and called Lisa.

"Hello," she said, answering the phone.

"Hey, baby! How's work?"

"Everything's fine. Something must be up, for me to get a phone call this early in the day. What's up, sweetie?" Lisa questioned.

"Girl, I don't know what you're talking about? Why can't I

simply want to talk to my baby?" Thomas replied in a conniving manner.

"Umm, sounds good, but I know better. Better yet, I know you. What's going on, boy? What do you want?"

"Nothing much, but I need a small favor."

"I knew it was something. What is it? I hope whatever it is, you don't need any money. If you do, I don't have any. I'm broke."

"No, it's nothing like that; it's about Derrick."

"Derrick? What about him?" Lisa asked, confused.

As Thomas was about to explain, someone knocked on his cubicle, trying to get his attention. "Hold on, baby." Thomas put the call on hold and turned to the gentleman waiting for him. "Hey, what's up?"

"What are you doing in this early? I thought you said that you'd be coming in late today," George, Thomas's editor, inquired.

"Yeah, I wasn't, but I needed to handle some things this afternoon. I decided to go ahead and get it out of the way."

"Is that right? Are you sure?"

Thomas gazed at him. "What else would it be?"

George shrugged. "I don't know. I thought it might have something to do with the detective in my office waiting to see you?"

Thomas looked puzzled. "Detective? What detective?"

"How am I supposed to know? He's waiting to speak to you; not me. I was about to give him your home address, but then I found out that you'd come in."

"Okay, give me a quick second and I'm on my way. If you don't mind, can you tell him that I'll be there in a minute?"

George nodded in agreement and walked off. Thomas picked the phone back up.

"Hey, baby, I can't talk to you right now. That was George. I have to go. They need me in a meeting."

"Wait a minute. At least tell me what this is all about?" Lisa questioned.

"It's only a meeting with George. It's nothing serious."

"No, not that. This thing with Derrick; what's up with that?"

"Oh, I can't get into detail right now about it. That's nothing serious either. Derrick needs a place to crash for a couple of days."

"Okay, and my next question is, what in the hell is wrong with the place where he pays rent?"

"Baby, look, I just told you that I can't really get into this right now. I'm sure you're going to want to give me an earful. I promise that I'll explain everything to you tonight when you get home. But right now, I have to go. I have a meeting."

"Tommy, I know you. I didn't say yes; we need to discuss this first so don't go making that boy any broken promises," Lisa said, reasserting her stance.

"Baby, I said that I'll explain everything to you tonight. We can talk about it then but, right now, I have to go. I love you."

"Fine; I love you, too," Lisa replied before she hung up the phone.

Thomas walked into George's office. Detective Peterson stood up from a chair.

George introduced the two of them. "Detective Peterson, this is Thomas Sharp."

Detective Peterson extended his hand to Thomas. Thomas shook it.

"I don't get too many detectives paying me a visit. This is surely a first. Did I get a promotion that I don't know about or some-thing, George, or did you forget that I'm a sports reporter?" Thomas asked jokingly.

They all shared a laugh.

"I'm not sure about that but I do have some questions for you on a certain matter and, hopefully, you'll have some helpful answers."

"Oh really, that's interesting. Questions about what?" Thomas asked.

"I was wondering the same thing," George said.

Detective Peterson turned toward George. "If you don't mind, can you please excuse us? I need to speak with Mr. Sharp alone."

George looked at Thomas to see if it was alright with him. Thomas didn't object. George headed to the door and then closed it behind him as he exited the room.

"So, detective, how can I help you?"

"Well, during the course of my investigation, your name came up and I was hoping you'd be able to shed some light on a few things."

"That's interesting. I'm not sure how I'd be any help with an investigation. What do you need from me?"

"I'm sure you probably know by now that Jose Benitez was killed earlier this morning."

"Yes, I found out when I came in."

"Is that so? Are you sure that's when you first found out?" Detective Peterson questioned.

"Yes, how else would I have found out?" Thomas shot back.

"I don't know; that's exactly what I'm trying to find out. How did you find out? I mean, I do find it a little puzzling that you called in to tell your editor that you were coming in late, but yet, here you are. My guess is you definitely knew something long before you got here today and only came in to see what others knew about the murder."

"That doesn't make sense. Again, I'm a sports reporter. I don't cover the local scene so I wouldn't need any information regarding a murder. That would be for the Metro section."

"Speaking of the local scene, I also find it very puzzling that you live in the exact neighborhood where the murder was committed, but yet you didn't find out anything until you arrived at work. Don't you find that odd, Mr. Sharp, or is that another one of the little funny coincidences?"

Thomas was caught off-guard by Detective Peterson's reply. It was obvious Detective Peterson knew quite a lot about Thomas. He wasn't expecting that.

"Well, in a sense, that is why I came in early, but it's not like you think. Because of all the chaos and commotion outside, I couldn't sleep, so I decided to come on in and get some work done early. Then I could have my afternoon to myself."

"Is that right? Well, what about your roommate?"

Thomas started choking. "Who?" He continued to cough.

"Are you okay?"

"Yeah, I'm fine. Thanks for asking. Something got stuck in my throat."

"Oh, okay. Well, as I was saying, what about your roommate?"

"Who?"

"Your roommate? The gentleman you share an apartment with," Detective Peterson said sarcastically.

Thomas regained his composure. "I didn't mean who, in that aspect, detective. I certainly know who my roommate is."

"I'm sorry. How did you mean it? I thought that was a pretty straightforward question. Please explain?"

"Detective, I meant who as in shocked that you would think my roommate would know anything about a murder. Derrick isn't that type of guy. He's far from it."

"When you say he isn't that type of guy, what type of guy would that be? I'm trying to see what he's heard or possibly saw. I didn't know a possible witness was a certain type of guy."

"I didn't mean it like that, detective. I meant that Derrick isn't the street type. He probably doesn't even know who Jose Benitez is, for that matter. He wouldn't be any help to your investigation because if he could, you would've already talked to him."

Detective Peterson started to smirk.

"Well, that's good to know, but I'd much rather hear that from him instead. You never know, anything could help at this point. Now how do I get in contact with him or where can I find him?"

"Detective, honestly, Derrick is a dead end. He doesn't know anything."

Frustration started to show on Detective Peterson's face. He paused before speaking, "Now you and I are both very intelligent men so let's not waste each other's time. You sound very confident that your roommate didn't witness or know anything, which leads me to believe that you're trying to protect him."

"May I speak?" Thomas asked.

"Sure."

"It's not that, detective. Yes, I can see where this is going and also leading. But, at the same time, I know my roommate. This is nowhere near up his alley. He isn't that type. If there was something he could've helped you with, trust me, you would've already known. I've already told you that. He's too dumb to keep information. He always wants to be helpful when he can. Also, I would've known by now. He would've told me and yet, I've heard nothing."

"Understood and thanks for clearing that up. Would you know by chance where I can find him?"

"Detective, again, you're wasting your time. Derrick is a dead end within your investigation," Thomas reiterated.

"Is that what he told you after you asked him if he knew anything?"

"Huh, no, I haven't talked to him."

"Then you aren't sure what he knows so, with that said, thanks but no thanks."

"Detective, maybe we got off on the wrong foot. I realize that you're trying to do your job and solve a case. I get that. I really do. That's why I'm trying to stop you from wasting your time; precious time at that. The first forty-eight hours are the most important, so I'm trying to save you some aggravation. You're barking up the wrong tree with Derrick."

"I appreciate your concern, but allow me to do my job and make that determination. Now, since you want to do favors and offer advice, allow me to do the same. I see exactly what you're doing. That's your boy and you're protecting him. I can't say that I wouldn't do the same thing if I were you; especially due to the identity of the murder victim and the people possibly involved. I get that. However, think about this. I found out about you and your boy. How long do you think it'll be before Omar finds out the same information? You say your boy isn't from the streets but it's obvious you know your way around a block or two. You know Omar has the city wrapped around his finger and exactly how he finds out information. So you also realize how this thing will go down the minute Omar finds out. These streets talk! Now if you really want to help your boy, allow me to help. I don't know what he knows or what he saw, but I can't help him if you won't allow it."

"Detective, I don't know what you're talking about!"

"I really would hate to see anything happen to either of you because you were trying to protect him. I see it day in and day out. The only way I can protect either of you is if you help me out."

"I'm sorry, was that a threat?" Thomas asked.

"No, it was far from one. I'm only trying to help you. Whether you want to believe it or not, it's a genuine concern. Once Omar catches wind of any information swirling around out here, he isn't going to come asking; you and I both know that. Now there are leaks within the department and it's obvious you also realize that. You don't really know if you can trust me or not. And to be honest with you, there's nothing I can tell you that'll get you to trust me. The only thing I can ask of you is please don't strip me of the opportunity to show you by doing my job."

"Let's say, hypothetically, that you're correct and my room-mate does know something. You can't guarantee his safety. Why would I talk him into signing up for a death sentence? What type of friend would that make me? Just like you think you can protect us, I'm sure that I can, so why would I take a risk on chances and hopes?"

"Thomas, you're trying to win a losing game. If you continue to try to play it your way, you'll lose and the next body I'll be standing over will either be yours, or your friend's. Please, allow me to help the both of you."

"How, detective? MPD doesn't have a good track record with keeping witnesses alive these days, with all their leaks. You've already admitted that much yourself."

"I'm not coming to you as a part of the MPD right now. I'm coming to you as Raymond Peterson. I'm coming to you as a man. Before I ever became a cop, I was a man first, and that's one thing I'll always be; even after the badge."

"Well, if I see Derrick, I'll ask him if he knows anything. If he does, we'll go from there."

Detective Peterson took out his business card. "Please have him give me a call. I promise you, I will protect him. I will protect the both of you. You have my word on that!"

Thomas took the card. "How many other dead witnesses were made that same promise?"

"None! I never make a promise that I can't keep," Detective Peterson replied. The look on his face said it all. It was evident he was dead serious and Thomas believed him. Detective Peterson didn't want to keep pressing the issue. He had somewhat gained Thomas's trust and didn't want to lose it by being overly eager. He got up and headed to the door. Before he exited, he turned back to Thomas. "I hope to be hearing from either of you very soon."

Thomas didn't reply. Detective Peterson left out of the office. Thomas continued to sit down, trying to figure out his next move. Nothing was going as he planned. The police had already found out who Derrick was and linked the two of them together. Detective Peterson was right; it wouldn't be long before word got back to Omar and then both him and his crew would be coming to look for the both of them next. Even though a part of him believed Detective Peterson, there was only but so much he could protect them from. Omar was too powerful in the District. He ran the city.

Thomas was more than sure Detective Peterson would either be tailing him himself or had put someone else on him. There was no way he could meet with Derrick. A thought came to him. Thomas got up and started to head back to his cubicle. As Thomas was leaving, George walked in.

"Hey, what was all that about?"

"Nothing really, I didn't have any helpful information."

Now intrigued, George asked, "Help how? What did he want your help with?"

"Since I live on Minnesota Avenue, he thought that I might have some informants who might've seen anything concerning the Jose Benitez murder. I told him that I don't hang out in the neighborhood or know anyone to ask. Unless it's something sports-related, I really don't bother with it."

"Shit, I could've told him that. You ask me, you love your job a little too much." They both started to laugh. "I wonder what made him think you would know anything about it or, better yet, how he even got your name. That's the part that seems so strange to me."

"I don't know. I wish that I could tell you, George. When you find out, you let me know; I surely would like to know the answer to that question. Well, I have some errands to run; if you need me, you can reach me on my cell. I'll still have my story in for the late edition so there's no need to worry and bug the hell out of me."

"You better, Thomas. I'm serious!"

Thomas walked out the office and closed the door behind him. George went to his desk and picked up the phone.

"Hey, it's me. I might have a possible lead on Jose's murder."

"How so?"

"A Detective Peterson came in to question one of my reporters."

"What's so special about that? I'm sure there were a lot of reporters at the scene, once it was called in. The detective might've only wanted to speak to your guy to give him a follow up or something. Next time, don't waste my time with such little information."

"Why would my sports reporter be on the scene of a murder investigation? Better yet, a sports reporter who happens to live on Minnesota Avenue. He wasn't giving him any follow-up. He was interviewing him as a possible witness."

"Well, is he? Did he see anything?"

"He told me that he didn't and, I'm guessing by how the detective left, he didn't tell him anything either, but he's acting very strange today. Something in my gut tells me that he knows something, but what that something is, is anyone's guess. Whatever it is, it most surely led that detective right to him. As a reporter, one of the things I first learned was where there's smoke there's fire."

"You might be on to something. I'll check into it. Where can I find him?"

"He lives at 5550 Minnesota Avenue in apartment two but my guess would be to head over to his girlfriend's house. She has an apartment over by First Street. He said he was still going to turn his story in and that's where he goes when he does his work off-site. His name is Thomas Sharp and his girlfriend's name is Lisa."

"Okay, thanks," Tito said.

"What about my payment?"

"You'll get your payment the same way you always do."

"I was thinking, seeing as how close to home this one is for you since it was Jose, my payment would be a little more, being as though this is very pertinent information."

"Point taken; it's done!" Tito said and then hung up the phone.

8

Omar's driver pulled the car up to the corner on Meigs Place. Omar looked around and noticed people standing around at the Trinidad playground. The word on the street was that's where he would be able to find Carlos. Even though he wasn't sure if Carlos was the one that he was looking for, this was the only move he had available to make. Just in case he was, he needed to put the word out there for him to hear it. It needed to be known that whoever was behind his nephew's murder would be dealt with severely.

Omar quickly surveyed his surroundings and noticed there were limited escape routes, in case something was to jump off. Tito walked up to the passenger side of the car and opened the door to let Omar out. Together, along with the driver and one other person, they walked to the playground courtyard to meet the men congregated there.

Carlos noticed them approaching. "Yo, we got trouble!"

Tony quickly turned around to see what Carlos was talking about. "Chill, it might not be anything at all. Don't overreact."

"Yeah, okay, but if they act a fool out here, please believe I'm letting each one of those niggas have it."

"Los, seriously, chill with all that," Tony said as they approached.

"Good day, gentleman. Which one of you is Carlos?" Omar asked.

"Who wants to know?" Tony replied.

Amused by Tony's reply, Tito started laughing. Omar gestured to Tito as if everything was kosher.

"I'm sure you know exactly who I am so please, spare me the childish games," Omar replied.

Carlos moved toward Omar. "What do you want with me?"

"Are you Carlos?" Tito asked defensively.

"Muthafucker, didn't I ask what you want with me? You tell me to stop playing games so please, don't play games with me. I wouldn't have asked that if it wasn't me. Now either you state your business or get the fuck off my block."

"Who do you think you're talking to?" Tito moved toward Carlos.

One of Carlos's boys was quick on the draw and pulled his pistol on Tito in defense of Carlos. In retaliation, Omar's driver and the fourth gentleman with Omar pulled out their guns. One was pointed at Carlos and the other at Tony. The scene was intense. Everyone was silent. The look in everyone's eyes said backing down wasn't an option.

"What are you going to do now, young fella?" Tito asked with a smile on his face. The fact that Carlos's man had him dead in his sights didn't even matter to him. Tito had no fear.

"Either you're going to tell me why you're asking for me or before your two little buddies there can let one loose on me, your brains will be splattered all over that park bench," Carlos answered.

That seemed to amuse Tito even more. "Confidence, I like that, young fella. I like that."

Omar moved in front of Tito. "Put your guns down please; this isn't the nature of our visit today. We come in peace, but in need of answers."

"I was always taught to never pull it out if I'm not going to use it," Carlos shot back.

"If you're going to quote a saying, then at least do it correctly. It's 'if you aren't prepared to use it, don't pull it out.' It looks pretty clear to me that everyone out here is prepared to do whatever is necessary, if need be." Omar paused in order to allow his words to sink in. "However, as I said, we come in search of answers so a gunfight won't solve anything."

"The last time I checked, I was the one who had two pistols pointing at me. So until I see that situation has changed, mine definitely will remain the same."

Omar waved for his men to put their guns away. They did as he ordered, but Carlos's acquaintance still had his pistol squarely pointed at Tito. Tony put his hand over the muzzle of his pistol. The guy put his pistol away.

"Now I'm going to ask you for the last time, what do you want with me?" Carlos asked.

"Some information is all we really need," Omar said.

"Okay, let's hear it," Tony said.

"Earlier today, my nephew was killed after visiting a female acquaintance of his."

"What does that shit have to do with me?" Carlos asked, getting impatient.

"Well, this young woman had your phone number in her cell phone. Now we are all men out here and it's possible that it was merely a coincidence but there is also that same possibility that it was by design. I'm not a man of assumptions or a guesser. And you, being a man, I figured that I would approach you like one to get an answer."

"First of all, never question my manhood. You're nothing but another nigga to me so don't think that I fear you in any way, shape, or form. I'm not one of these little bitch-ass niggas you have running around in these streets scared. I don't fear anyone.

Second, I don't know why your nephew's girl would have my number; I don't know the bitch. I know my sex game is on one thousand but you might be giving me way too much credit," Carlos replied as he turned to give his boy some dap.

"So, are you saying you don't know Maria and that wasn't your number?" Tito asked.

"I'm really starting to believe something is wrong with your hearing. I already said that but, for you, I'll repeat myself one more time. Naw, sorry, that name doesn't ring a bell. The number you found, it wasn't my number."

"Yeah, okay, we'll see about that." Tito pulled out his cell phone and started to dial the mysterious number. Tito heard the phone ringing through his receiver, but no one's phone was ringing out loud.

"Let me guess; you're supposedly calling my phone?" Carlos grinned. He reached into his pocket and pulled out his phone. "Just in case you thought my phone might've been on vibrate or silent."

There was no call coming through to Carlos's cell phone. The number wasn't his.

Tito closed his phone and put it away. Carlos stared at Tito like he was crazy.

"Are there any more little demonstrations, or is that it? I already told you, I don't know the bitch. You've got the wrong guy. I don't have anything more to tell you."

Omar jumped in. "You possibly are correct. Maybe we do have the wrong person and if so, then an apology for the misunderstanding is due. But if I don't, please understand this is my nephew we are talking about. My blood! I will not rest until—"

Tony cut him off. "My man has already told you on more than one occasion that he doesn't know her, so your threats aren't needed nor paid any attention, Mr. Benitez."

Omar cracked a smile. "So you do know who I am? That's good; you have the proper understanding of exactly what I'm capable of if I find out that you're lying."

"Man, fuck this!" Carlos shouted out in frustration. Tony quickly grabbed him, trying to calm him down.

"No, this nigga thinks he's God or something!"

Tony gave him a stern look. Carlos stopped with his tirade. Tony turned back to Omar. "Honestly speaking, who you are is irrelevant. What you have done in the past is just that, the past. Time always changes things and if you keep thinking we're soft or you're going to intimidate us, not only are you sadly mistaken, you'll quickly see how much times have changed."

Omar continued to still wear the same smile on his face. He turned to Tito. "Ahh, youth. You have to love it." Tito smiled back at him. Omar then turned back toward Tony. "When you're young, you think that you're invincible. Youth blinds you to how vulnerable you really are. Now, with age, that's where you become wiser."

"What the fuck does that have to do with anything?" Carlos asked.

"Keep running off at the mouth and whether you had something to do with my nephew's murder or not, you'll quickly find out exactly what it has to do with everything. It's one thing to not be soft, it takes something to be a man, but it doesn't take anything at all to be a stupid idiot."

"You and all these fucking riddles and shit. Look, all this talking is really dead to me. Do what you have to do?" Carlos replied.

"Right now, I have more pressing issues to take care of; however, you know where I stand."

"And you know where we stand as well. Now, if there's nothing else, please get the fuck off of my block," Tony stated vehemently.

"You gentleman enjoy the rest of your short-lived lives. May you be blessed within them."

"Short-lived, huh? Yeah, please believe I take that as a threat," Carlos said.

"Take it how you want. How you take anything I say, I care nothing about. Good day, gentlemen." Omar turned around and headed back to his car. The driver and other gentleman followed behind him. Tito looked at Carlos and cracked a smile.

"Until we meet again," Tito said and then followed behind Omar.

Once Omar's crew was no longer within distance to hear anything, Tony looked at Carlos and shook his head.

"What?" Carlos questioned.

"What do you mean, what? This was supposed to be something low-key. Low-key means no damn clues; no trail to use. How the fuck did they find us? That's what."

"They didn't; they found a number to someone named Carlos. Which I might add, I proved wasn't me. Come on now, Tony, think about. They don't even know if Carlos is who they're really looking for. All they know is that he was fucking Jose's bitch."

"I should've known. I don't know why I didn't put two and two together."

"What are you talking about now?" Carlos asked Tony.

"That's why you wanted to hit Jose. The two of you were fucking the same chick. Now it all makes sense."

"Obviously it doesn't because Maria has nothing to do with this. She never hid him from me. I knew she was his bitch from jump. Shit, she used to brag all the time about how she helped him move product. She was no more to me than she was to him; some ass. I chose him because he was the easiest Eastside Riderz to get. I'm sick of them thinking they run the city and it's time for a new day. Them bitches don't run me. Everyone is scared to bring the war to them. Well, not us. I can't believe you sitting here about to trip off this bullshit. Just like I got to Jose's bitch, we got to Jose, and soon enough, we'll get to Omar, too. We're going to touch all them bitches, please believe," Carlos replied.

Tony wasn't buying Carlos's reply. There was more to it than what Carlos was letting on to.

"What?" Carlos asked as Tony continued to stare at him.

"Nothing," Tony replied.

"Don't tell me nothing. You're standing there staring at me with that blank-ass look on your face. Just get the shit off your chest."

"If you have us going to war over some pussy—"

Carlos quickly cut Tony off. "How long have you known me?" Carlos was getting defensive about Tony's suggestion.

"What does that have to do with anything?"

"You've known me since we were both kids running around the damn playground together. In all that time, there isn't one bitch that you can name that I've ever let interfere with business. You, of all people, should know that I go from one to the next one. I don't give a shit about none of these bitches. I never have. Money is what makes me cum!"

Tony didn't reply.

Carlos continued, "Exactly! You can't say shit, can you? Because you know, there isn't one chick you can name so now, all of a sudden, a chick you knew nothing about had me so wrapped up that I'm willing to go to war with arguably the most feared crew in all of D.C. Come on, that don't even make any sense and you know it. This is strictly business; nothing more, and nothing less!"

"Okay, maybe so, but, still, you should've told me about her."

"If I would've told you, then you wouldn't have wanted to hit Jose."

"You're right and that's because the plan was to do everything under the radar. Look where the connection has us now, under suspicion. Yeah, he still doesn't know that it's us but the connection is what has him jockeying us."

"Honestly, we're more under the radar now than before. Before, Omar didn't know who was behind anything. He still doesn't but now he thinks we aren't, so we're in the clear."

"Do you really believe we're in the clear? Hell no, the only thing we've done is bought a little more time."

"Look, what's done is done. We can't go back and change anything. I chose Jose. Maria helped us get Jose. We hit Jose; game on! Now, instead of sitting here complaining about how we got into the game, you should be concentrated on how we're going to win it."

"I'm always focused on the next move so we can achieve the number one prize. But that still doesn't change the fact that I don't like surprises and I just got hit with one hell of one."

"Understood. Now, what do we do about these niggas before they do start to piece shit together?" Carlos asked.

"My guess is we really only have one move and that's to stick to the original plan. The only difference is we need to accelerate it a bit."

"I'm lost, how did you come up with that?"

"Think about it. They know about Maria, so it's safe to assume they paid her a visit first. She must didn't give us up, or Omar wouldn't have come asking questions. The questions were only to gauge our reaction to the situation. So since she had nothing to offer, then more than likely, she's dead but yet we're still alive. That's what bothers me. The logical move would've been to kill us both and not take our word and risk being wrong. That's what I would've done if I was in his situation and you would have, too."

"But we're talking about a man who lost his nephew. His own

flesh and blood. People don't think logically under those types of circumstances. People make rash decisions that lead to mistakes in judgment. That could be why we're alive."

"Anything is possible, but I doubt it. We're alive for a reason. He has something up his sleeve. Whatever it is, we don't have time to figure it out. We need to get to Omar," Tony replied.

"Now you're talking my language," Carlos said excitedly.

"Okay, Omar's the brains of the business, but Tito's the brains of the muscle. There's no way in hell we even come close to getting Omar, with Tito alive. We have to take Tito out. Plus, if anyone is coming after us, you know that's who it's going to be. By killing Tito, we eliminate two birds with one stone."

"I'm game but won't Omar go into hiding the minute he finds out his muscle has been hit? How will we get at him then?"

"We don't give him the time to go into hiding. We put our man on Tito and the minute we get the word he took care of him, we hit Omar. That's the only way."

"Sounds like a plan to me. Let's call up your man and get him on Tito. I'll get someone on Omar so the minute Tito goes down, Omar goes down, too."

✠ ✠ ✠

Tito and Omar reached the cars in the parking lot. As Omar got in his car, Tito did the same.

"What do you want to do about those two?" Tito asked, pointing to the courtyard where Carlos and Tony stood.

"It's obvious that they're involved, but I find it hard to believe that they have the resources to pull something like this off by themselves. They're getting help and we need to find out where that help is coming from."

"So you really think it's them? The cell phone number wasn't even his, though."

"That's only a minor detail; probably only smoke and mirrors. He could have more than one phone and the number Maria had went to his other phone. The number meant nothing. Their body language and attitude are what said it all. There's not a doubt in my mind, my friend. The only reason why they're still breathing is because I want everyone who had anything to do with my nephew's murder. No one is getting a pass on this one. Anyone who had anything to do with it will suffer the same consequence; regardless of what role they played."

"Understood. Well, I got a lead on a witness. It seems he works for the paper. How do you want to play this?" Tito asked.

"That's perfect. Go see what he knows and then we'll deal with our new friends. We might need to put them on the back burner for now. I don't want to leave a single stone unturned. I'm not certain if either of them are the shooter. I didn't get that vibe so maybe this witness can give us more information on that."

"Not a problem, but what if we find out that it wasn't them who put the hit on Jose and they really didn't have anything to do with the murder? Do you still want me to take care of them?"

"If there's a slim chance that I'm wrong and they aren't involved, then regardless, they still need to be dealt with. The two things they lack both concern me. They lack fear and respect and have replaced it with ambition. In our trade, youth with ambition is always a problem. Even if they aren't an immediate problem, it won't be long before they'll become one. We need to put an end to them before they even get started. But first things first; pay a visit to this witness and after you find out all you need to, make sure he isn't a witness for anyone else," Omar said.

9

Thomas stood outside his building pacing back and forth, thinking about what his next move needed to be. If the police were able to find him, it would only be a matter of time before the Eastside Riderz would be the next ones knocking on the door, looking for him. He wasn't even the one who witnessed anything, Derrick was, but he wasn't going to sit around and wait for anyone from Eastside to visit him and try to explain his case. The minute they found out how useless he was, they would cut their losses and he'd be disposed of.

Then he thought that maybe, if he brokered the information Derrick knew for their lives to be spared, that might be the trick to come out of the situation alive. But just as quickly as the thought entered his mind, it exited. Regardless, whether Omar agreed or not, ultimately, he would still kill them. No matter how much help Derrick could provide them, both of them would be potential witnesses regarding whatever revenge Omar had planned. He surely wouldn't leave them alive to testify later on down the road. There was no exit. His initial plan was all they could do. Just lay low until the heat blew over and they fell off everyone's radar.

A car pulled up to the curb where Thomas was standing. He quickly got into the car.

"Hey, baby. What was so urgent that you had me leave work to come and get you?" Lisa asked, concerned.

"Right now, just drive and get me out of here."

Without hesitation, Lisa pulled off. They sat in the car in silence as Lisa continued to drive. Thomas kept turning around to make sure no one was following them. Lisa's nerves started to get the best of her. Thomas wasn't acting normal. There was something definitely wrong and her curiosity was getting the best of her.

"Baby, please tell me what the hell is going on," Lisa pleaded.

"I need you to do me a favor. I need you to go to Lucky Strikes and get Derrick. I'm going to head to your house and I want you to bring him there. Better yet, it would probably be better if we went somewhere else. If they found me at work, then your house might not be the best spot to head to either."

Lisa pulled the car over. She couldn't take it anymore. Derrick was speaking in riddles that she couldn't solve. She needed solid and clear answers and she needed them fast.

"What are you doing?" Thomas asked.

"Something is going on and I've asked you repeatedly what it is while all you've done is repeatedly ignored me. Now we are going to sit right here and I won't move this car not one inch until you tell me what the hell is going on."

While Lisa was talking, Thomas turned around again to see if they were being followed. As he suspected, a car pulled over a couple of lengths behind them.

"Shit!" he yelled. He turned back toward Lisa. "Sweetie, please, not now. Trust me; the less you know, the better. I don't want you in any danger either. It's bad enough that things are as bad as they are now. I wouldn't be able to live with myself if anything ever happened to you because of me."

"Tommy, please stop and talk to me. What are you talking about? Baby, you aren't making any sense and it's starting to scare me."

"Please, can you just listen to me and not fight me on this."

"What is going—"

"Lisa, drive the fucking car!" Thomas yelled.

Startled, Lisa jumped. Thomas was totally out of character for himself. Whatever was going on, it had to have been something serious. And though she badly wanted to know what specifically it was that was going on, she didn't want to make matters worse by sitting there. Lisa put the car back in drive and pulled off.

Thomas turned back around to verify that his prior suspicion was correct. This time Lisa also looked in the rearview mirror, wanting to see exactly what Thomas was looking for. Both of them noticed the same car pulling off right as they did. It was obvious they were being followed. Panic read all on Lisa's face. At that moment, she started to understand how serious the situation was and why Thomas was acting that way.

Thomas noticed how fast Lisa was driving. It was obvious to him that she realized that someone was following them. He put his hand on her knee, trying to calm her nerves.

"I'm sorry for snapping at you. I shouldn't have, but please slow down. I don't want them to pull us over."

"Who?" Lisa questioned.

"The police. That's who's following us. It's the police."

"Why are the police following you?"

Thomas knew that she'd continue to ask questions but he didn't want to tell her too much.

"I'm not sure if you heard, but there was a murder around my neighborhood earlier this morning and they think that I witnessed it. I tried to tell them that I didn't see anything, but since it's a high-profile case, they're simply being extra cautious."

"Thomas, that doesn't make any sense; I wasn't born yesterday. They're following you for a reason."

"I told you why, baby; they believe that I witnessed a murder."

"What murder?"

"Jose Benitez," Thomas replied.

The look on Lisa's face said it all. At that very moment, what she thought was serious had been taken to the next level. The police were more than likely tailing them for the Eastside Riderz. Omar Benitez had more police working for him than any other crime figure in the city. The apprehension that she initially felt was now gone. She wanted to help Thomas in any way that she could.

"So what do you want me to do?" Lisa asked.

"Obviously, now you see why I can't go home. I'm sure they know exactly where I live. Derrick is so green to everything. I don't want him to get caught up in this. That's why I asked you if he could crash at you house for a bit until everything cooled off and either the police found the killer or hopefully, the person who really witnessed everything came forward."

"I understand completely. That's fine, baby; both of you can stay with me. So where am I taking you now?"

Thomas didn't reply; he sat there contemplating the next smart move. Hiding out at Lisa's place was no longer an option. He wasn't sure if Detective Peterson was following them, or if it was one of Omar's crooked cops. Either way, he couldn't chance leading them to Derrick.

"I've got it. I'm about to get out of the car so slow it down."

"What, for what, baby? You said we need to get to Derrick. I don't think that's smart to split up."

"We have to. I want you to go ahead and head to Lucky Strikes and meet Derrick. That's where he is. While you're doing that, I'm going to lose the police on the train. It's me that they want, so they'll stop tailing you and follow me. I'm going to head over to your house, pack up a bag, and then we'll all meet up later tonight."

Confused, Lisa asked, "Why change up everything now? Why not just do what you wanted to earlier and stay at my house until everything blows over?"

"Because the situation has changed; I'm sure they've run your license plate by now. It won't be long before they're staking out your place. Your place is going to be as hot as if we stayed at our own."

"So if we aren't staying at my place, then where are we going?" Lisa asked.

"We have a better shot, if we head across the line. If we stay in D.C., we're as good as dead. Omar has people all over the city. Let's head to Virginia, or maybe Maryland, get a hotel room, and sit for a few days. He has his hands in both those areas also, but at least we'll have more of a fighting chance there than what we'll have if we stay in D.C."

"I can't not go to work, baby. I can't miss days like that," Lisa replied.

"Neither can I. I don't know how we're going to work that out but first things first; let's cross this obstacle and then we'll think the rest of it out later. I'd rather lose a job versus my life. Now pull over right here; I need to ditch these cops and you need to get to Derrick before they find him. Let's meet at the Motel 6 in Camp Springs off Allentown Road. It's very low-key and it's by Andrews Air Force Base. I doubt if Omar has any contacts in that area."

"Do you really think this is a good idea?"

"Baby, right now, it's the only idea. Come on; I need you to be strong. We're going to get through this but don't be out here careless. I need you to be very careful! Make sure you're very conscious and paying close attention to your surroundings. Pull over right there."

Lisa pulled the car over. This time the police drove right past them and then pulled over a couple of cars in front of them instead of behind them.

"What do you want me to do if they keep following me?" Lisa asked.

"I doubt they will, but if by chance they do, then leave the car downtown. I'll come back and get it for you later. I'll leave them behind somewhere, if they sit on the car and then follow me. Just park it on the street and after you get Derrick, y'all catch the subway to the Branch Avenue subway station and catch a cab to the motel. Don't you try to lose them driving."

"Baby, I'm scared. I don't have a good feeling about this."

"Everything is going to work out; watch. Don't be scared, sweetie. I need you to be strong right now. I told you, we're going to get through this. This whole situation is going to work itself out. Trust me; we'll be fine. Everything will blow over by Monday. This is too big of a case for people in the streets not to start talking and for Omar not to find out who killed Jose. Even if word doesn't get back to Omar, the police definitely will have extra motivation to find out who did it. Either way, once the killer is caught, everything else will go back to normal. Let's get through right now and make it to tomorrow; then we'll deal with the next day. That's all we can do, is try to take all of this one day at a time. I need you to be focused on the right now; okay, baby?"

"Okay, baby, I will. I want you to be careful, too. I love you," Lisa said.

"I love you, too," Thomas replied. He gave her a kiss and then opened the car door and got out.

She rolled down the window. Thomas leaned his head back into the car.

"Wait until you see them get out of the car and follow me. There are two of them in the car. If they both get out, then drive off. If only one gets out, still drive off but make sure you pay attention to see if the other cop is following you."

"What if he does follow me; then what?"

"Then you do the same thing I'm doing and get on the subway. Park the car somewhere downtown, catch the train to Derrick, and then get back on the train and head to the Branch Avenue station."

Lisa nodded in agreement. Thomas started to walk up the street. One of the officers noticed Thomas walking and did just what Thomas thought he'd do. He quickly got out of the car and started to follow behind him. Lisa patiently waited for his partner to pull off, but he didn't. It didn't look like he was going to make the situation as easy as Lisa had hoped. It looked like he was going to continue to sit there waiting to see what Lisa's next move would be. Then, suddenly, she saw his car pull out of his parking spot and race down the street with his siren on.

Lisa realized that the coast was clear. Without hesitation, she pulled off and went in the opposite direction. It might take her a little longer to get to Derrick but she didn't want to chance being followed. With the way the second officer had pulled off, something had to have happened.

Thomas was in a full out sprint running down M Street in Southeast D.C. He wasn't far from the First District precinct. Though he doubted the officer chasing him would call in for assistance, he also didn't want to take the chance of how things would turn out if he did. He needed to get off the streets and fast, but also, at the same time, lose his tail. The only way was to make it to the subway station and avoid them on the train.

Thomas noticed the sound of a siren in the distance. The siren was faint but started to get more distinct as it got closer and closer. Thomas cut up a side street and cut through the housing development. With all the new construction going on in the neighborhood, he was going to have to be crafty with his disappearing act.

Thomas cut into the Safeway parking lot as if he were going to make his way to the Waterfront subway station. It only made sense to lose them there. The officer chasing behind him broke off his pursuit and took a shortcut to the Waterfront station, trying to beat Thomas to the punch. Thomas noticed he was no longer being chased and realized that something was up. Instead of heading to Waterfront, he cut up Sixth Street.

The officer got to the Waterfront subway station in no time. He looked around, making sure Thomas hadn't already beaten him there. Once he didn't see him outside, he headed to the subway platform to meet him there.

Thomas continued up Sixth Street until he reached D Street. The only problem with his detour to the subway was that he was now around more government buildings. He didn't want to continue running and bring unneeded attention to himself. However, if the police were still on his tail, it would be a lot easier to catch him while he was walking. Either way, he had to risk it. He slowed down but kept a steady walking pace as he walked past the Department of Housing and Urban Development. The closer he got to the L'Enfant Plaza subway station, the more nervous he became.

Thomas didn't know what to expect. Anything was possible and he didn't want to assume that he was in the clear. Thomas entered the station and jumped on the train heading back toward the Branch Avenue station in Maryland. Though the train would pass the Waterfront subway station on its way back into Maryland, Thomas figured if the officer did go to the Waterfront subway station instead, he would never guess to look on an incoming train for him.

As the train pulled into the station, surely enough, both of the officers were standing there looking around the subway platform for him. Thomas ducked down, trying to avoid their detection. The officers kept looking toward the escalator that was bringing all the commuters down to the platform. Never did they even bother to look over at the oncoming trains. The door chime sounded, notifying all passengers that the train doors were about to close. The doors closed and then the train pulled off. Thomas breathed a quick but short-lived sigh of relief.

10

Derrick was a nervous wreck. The whole situation seemed like a scene from out of a movie instead of his life. He needed something to calm his nerves and he figured a drink was the perfect solution. He only needed one to take the edge off and relax, but one drink quickly turned into number three and he was just as nervous as he had been before he had started drinking.

The waitress approached. "Would you like another drink?"

"I don't think I should; I've had enough," Derrick replied.

The waitress sat down next to him. "Is there something wrong?"

"Something? No, I wouldn't say something. It's more like *everything* is wrong right about now."

"Well, if you ask me, I say don't allow it to get to you. No woman is worth your happiness."

Derrick started laughing. "What makes you think my troubles have anything to do with a woman?"

"That usually is the case. Most of the time a man's troubles start and end right there. Especially the brothers that come in here; it almost always has something to do with a woman," the waitress replied.

"You know what, I don't even doubt it. However, my case would be one of those rare occasions you'd have; my troubles have nothing to do with a woman. Shoot, I wish it was over a woman.

Compared to what I'm dealing with right now, that would be a walk in the park. I could handle that with no problem but this, yeah, this is a different beast all in itself."

"Baby, are you sure you don't want to talk about it? I'm not a therapist or anything, but I'm a very good listener. Sometimes talking about our problems is the best remedy."

"No, I'm cool, but thanks. I really appreciate the offer." The waitress didn't want to be overly aggressive. She got up from off the barstool. "Well, if you change your mind and decide that you want to talk about it, I'm here," she said as she placed his drink down in front of him.

"Thanks, but I'm good. I don't need another drink, sweetie."

"I know what you said, but this one is on me." She gave him a wink of the eye and then walked off.

Derrick didn't even have the energy to fight it. With all that was going on, he probably needed as many drinks as possible. He had people who were trying to kill him and no one he could turn to in order to save him. Derrick mumbled to himself. "Hey, if I'm going to face death, I might as well do it drunk. You are right! Thanks for the drink. Shit, as a matter of fact, I probably should get another one."

Derrick looked toward the door and noticed someone who resembled Lisa entering the bowling alley. He wasn't sure if it was the alcohol making him delusional, or if it was really Lisa. He had to have been seeing things. What would Lisa be doing at Lucky Strikes? Derrick downed his drink and tried to shake his delusions off. Whoever the woman was, she noticed Derrick sitting at the bar and started to walk straight toward him. He started to think that maybe, he wasn't crazy. Maybe it was Lisa. The closer she got, the more and more he became certain it actually was Lisa.

"Hey, Derrick."

"Hey, what are you doing here? Where is Thomas?"

"The police were following us earlier and he asked me to come and get you. He didn't want to bring them to you."

The waitress noticed Derrick had company and made her way back over to him with another drink. She set it down on the bar. "Can I get you anything?" she asked Lisa.

"No thank you," Lisa replied.

"Are you sure?" the waitress asked.

"Pay her no attention; go ahead and bring her a drink, too. But make sure it's something fruity," Derrick said. He paused and then took a real good look at the waitress. "Have I told you how cute you are?" Derrick flirted with the waitress.

Lisa could tell that Derrick was drunk. Any other time, he was as shy as he could be around women. If they started talking to him, he wasn't rude or anything. He would engage them in casual conversation but he never tried to aggressively flirt with one as he was with the waitress.

"I said that I'm good and please believe me, I don't need anything fruity. I don't drink fruity drinks. It's obvious that your boy hasn't schooled you yet on me."

"Why would he need to school me on what you drink? That's none of my business," Derrick said, dismissing Lisa's comment. He turned his attention back toward the waitress. He continued, "I'm sorry that I didn't catch your name earlier."

"It's Cherrie," the waitress replied.

"Well, Cherrie, please get my friend a shot since she's a big girl and, also, your number would be extra nice so we can finish our talk from earlier at a later time."

"Not a problem with the shot and I'll look forward to the call," Cherrie said and then walked off.

"Derrick, we don't have time for all of this. We need to get out of here," Lisa said while looking at the door.

"Just relax! I ordered you a drink and she hasn't even given me her number yet. We're going to sit here and down these drinks and wait for Thomas."

"Derrick, Thomas isn't coming. I told you, he didn't want to draw the police to you so he sent me to come and get you."

"Oh yeah, that's right; you did say that. Well, give me a minute. I need to sit here and think this thing through."

Lisa started laughing. Though this was no time for laughter, the fact that Derrick thought he'd be able to figure out a solution to this problem tickled her. Derrick was the last person anyone would go to for advice for something hood-related.

"What's so damn funny?" Derrick asked.

"Nothing is funny, Derrick."

"You surely are laughing, though."

"Derrick, please, let's get out of here. Thomas is working on everything. He'll come up with something. Come on; let's go before someone spots us in here."

"I am a grown ass man. I don't need Thomas to figure anything out for me. This is my damn situation. I can handle my own problems. Plus, who the hell would spot us at a bowling alley? Just relax; you're too uptight. Where is Cherrie with your damn drink?"

"Wait a minute! What do you mean by your own problems?" Lisa was confused. As far as she knew, this had all started because the police suspected that Thomas knew something about Jose's murder.

"Huh, what do you mean?" Derrick replied.

"You said that you can handle your own problems. What did you mean by that? I thought the police were following Thomas because they thought he witnessed a murder."

"What! What murder?" Derrick asked, trying to play things off. The alcohol didn't have him as sharp as he'd normally be. He assumed that since Lisa was there to pick him up and she had witnessed the police following Thomas, that Thomas had told her everything that was going on. Instead of assuming, Derrick realized that he should've found out exactly what Lisa was privy to prior to saying anything.

"Don't try it, Derrick. Now tell me what the hell is going on?"

"Lisa, first of all, you need to calm down. Second, I don't know what you're talking about. I was fired from my job earlier today. I thought that was what you were talking about. I don't need Thomas to figure out my problems; I can handle that myself. Now what the hell are you talking about? What murder?"

Lisa didn't know whether to believe Derrick or not; his reply did sound very convincing. It was damn near believable. Lisa started to wonder if she had told Derrick too much. Maybe Thomas didn't want Derrick to know what was going on because of how naïve he was and he probably would want them to go to the police, thinking they could help in a situation like this. The waitress approached the two of them and gave Lisa her shot and Derrick her number.

"Please, don't hesitate to use that either," she said.

"Oh, please believe me, I won't," Derrick replied. The waitress walked off. Derrick put her number in his pocket and turned to Lisa. "What's going on, Lisa?"

Lisa downed her shot. "Okay, look, I don't know much but the police are under the impression that Thomas witnessed Jose Benitez's murder earlier this morning and now they're looking for him."

"Is that what he told you?"

"Yes. Why; is there more?"

"I don't know. Thomas asked me to meet him here and while I was here, I decided to have a couple of drinks because of what happened to me. So what's the so-called plan?"

"I told you, I don't know much either. Thomas didn't tell me the plan. He was worried. I didn't understand all that was going on at the time, until I saw us being followed. Then, I started to understand how serious everything was. So, at the time, I didn't really question him like I should have to find out more specifics."

"So what happened? How do you know it was the police following you?"

"When Thomas got out of the car and went up the street, one of them followed behind him on foot and the other sat and waited. Then, not too long after they were gone, the one that was waiting turned his siren on and darted up the street like a bat out of hell."

"Shit! So what are we going to do?"

"We are going to get out of here and meet Thomas at the Motel 6 by Andrews Air Force Base and then we'll go from there."

"Is that where he is now?" Derrick asked.

"No, he's going to meet us there. He needed to go by my place first to get some things."

"Get what? That doesn't make any sense. Yeah, you are right. We need to get out of here, but we're not going to any Motel 6. We need to head over to your place."

"Derrick, Thomas said to meet him at the motel."

"I don't give a shit what he said. Y'all might think I'm slow, but I'm not dumb. The minute they got behind you, they ran your license plates. What makes you think if he lost them, they wouldn't think to go to your house, under the assumption that that's where y'all would meet up? You're the only lead they have to find him again. They're probably sitting on your place right now, and my best friend is walking into a trap. I'm not going to a fucking motel and leaving him hanging stranded. Fuck that!" Derrick took some money out of his pocket and threw it on the bar, along with the waitress's tip. "Now, let's get out of here and get this show on the road. I'm not about to leave my man out there."

✠ ✠ ✠

Thomas walked into Lisa's dark apartment. The daylight was starting to break outside so there was no natural sunlight coming in through the closed shades to lighten up her place. Thomas clicked on the light switch and jumped back. Tito was sitting in Lisa's living room with his pistol aimed squarely at Thomas. He stood there, frozen.

"Thomas, I presume?" Tito asked.

"Who are you?" Thomas replied nervously.

"Who I am isn't important! Why don't you come have a seat?" Tito instructed.

Thomas did as he was told. He went over and sat opposite Tito on the couch. Thomas's nerves were at full tilt. Whoever this was, he wasn't a cop.

"Relax." Tito sensed how uneasy Thomas was.

"It's kind of hard to, with a gun pointed at me. Look, if this is a robbery, please, go ahead and take whatever it is you came to get or need. It's really not that serious."

"Do I look like some crackhead needing to commit a robbery? Please don't insult me."

"I'm sorry. I wasn't trying to insult you. I just don't want any trouble. I just—"

Tito cut him off. "Look, my friend, I need a little bit of information and then I'm out of your hair. I heard that you might be able to help me solve a seemingly pressing issue."

Confused, Thomas didn't know how to reply. He sat there, waiting for Tito to fill in the blanks. However, Tito continued to stare at him until Thomas finally opened his mouth, "And how can I do that?"

"Earlier today, there was a murder over on Minnesota Avenue that you might've witnessed."

Thomas quickly jumped. "I don't know anything about that."

Tito picked his pistol back up. "Now, before you answer, I want you to think long and hard about where a lie will get you over simply coming out and being honest with me. I can be the nicest person in the world, but if I need to be something else, that I can also be. Now, are you sure that's the answer you want to stick with?"

Thomas recognized that his life was now in jeopardy. If he acted like he knew nothing at all, things probably wouldn't go well for him. He needed to give Tito something, but what to give him troubled him. He didn't know what to say. There was no way he was going to give his best friend up. He needed to think of something and he needed to think of it fast.

Tito finished, "So, I'll ask again, is there anything about the murder that you would like to tell me?"

"All I know is that Jose Benitez was murdered. I don't know by who or nothing like that; just the fact that he was murdered today."

"So why did you try to act like you knew nothing at all?"

"Because, this is Jose Benitez we're talking about. Who wants their name associated in any way with his murder? I know all about the Eastside Riderz and Omar Benitez. I definitely didn't want any association to his nephew's murder; especially since I don't know anything about it."

"Body language never lies, my friend. Your body language tells me how worried you are. If you know nothing, then what is there to be worried about? You see, your body language is telling a different story than your mouth."

"Honestly, if I seem nervous, it's because of this situation right here. It has nothing to do with me knowing or not knowing anything. This isn't something that I'm used to. It's not every day I have someone threatening to kill me."

"Good point; however, I've already told you that you hold your own life within your hands." Tito paused. "If you know nothing about the murder, then why did the police question you earlier? What purpose would they have for you?"

At that very moment, Thomas almost shit his pants. This man knew far too much about him. Not only did this person know that he'd be at Lisa's house, but he also knew that he'd already been questioned by the police. Thomas assumed that he also knew about Derrick as well.

"They wanted to know pretty much the same thing you do. Since I lived right by the scene of the crime, they were asking possible witnesses in the area if they saw anything."

"Really, I find that quite odd since you're one of the few potential witnesses they questioned. Not to mention the fact that even though your apartment is in the area, it's definitely not in the immediate vicinity. So, why would they be questioning you, unless they were pretty sure there was something you could do to help them with their case?"

"I honestly do not know. You might not believe me but I'm telling the truth. I don't know anything! Please, don't do anything to me. I don't know what to tell you. I don't know anything. If you committed the murder, I know nothing about it. You don't have to silence me. Please, don't hurt me."

Tito was now thrown off. If Thomas had witnessed the murder, then why would he think that he was the murderer? It was obvious Thomas hadn't witnessed anything. He was under the impression that Tito had killed Jose and was now there to shut him up. So if Thomas didn't witness the murder, then why did the police want to question him? Maybe Thomas was only the stepping stone to the real missing piece.

"What exactly did the police ask you?" Tito questioned.

Totally not thinking about the correct response, Thomas quickly answered the question. "They asked if I or my roommate knew anything about the murder. That's it. I told them that we didn't and then he left."

"Roommate, what roommate? You have a roommate?"

Thomas quickly calmed himself, realizing the mistake he'd made. Derrick was the one everyone really wanted to speak to. He held the answers to all of the questions. The mystery man knew so much, Thomas had assumed that he also knew that he had a roommate.

"Yes, I do but he was home with me when everything went down this morning. He knows the same amount about this situation as I do; nothing. Actually, he knows less because he doesn't even know who Mr. Benitez is."

"Really? I find that very interesting, that the police would question someone who knew nothing about nothing. Why would they even come to you, at your job at that? Everything you are saying doesn't seem right. Then not only does your roommate know nothing, but he knows less than you and you are jittery."

"I told you; I'm just very nervous."

"I believe you," Tito said.

Thomas started to relax. For once, he started to feel at-ease.

"However, what I don't believe is that both of you know nothing at all. That is what I don't believe. So tell me where I can find your roommate and I'm out of here."

"I don't know. I'm not sure where he is."

"You see, I thought we had a good understanding about the truth versus a lie and the consequences that one would bring."

"I do understand but, I don't know where he is. I don't," Thomas repeated.

Tito started to rub his chin. Thomas wasn't sure what was next. He was praying that Tito believed him. Tito stood up out of his seat and walked toward Thomas.

"When was the last time you saw him?"

"I saw him this morning before I left the house. I was running late so we didn't really have time to talk this morning. Last night, he told me that he had some errands to run, but he never said what they were or where he was going. I'm telling you; he doesn't know anything. He was still in the house when I left the house this morning, so how could he? We both were home when everything went down."

Tito paused, considering all that Thomas had said. Thomas's reply was so fast, he was trying to catch his breath. Before he could, with one swift blow, Tito knocked him to the floor. Blood started to pour from Thomas's mouth. Tito now had his gun pointed directly at Thomas again. The fear that had briefly subsided was now full tilt.

"I'm telling you the truth. I don't know where he is. Please, don't kill me."

Without saying a word, Tito shot Thomas in his right leg. Thomas quickly grabbed his leg and let out a loud scream.

"The more you lie, the more pain you will feel," Tito said. "Now, where can I find your roommate?"

The burning sensation shot throughout Thomas's body. He couldn't concentrate. He didn't hear a word Tito had said. All of his attention was on his gunshot wound. Tito started to become irritated. He put the barrel of his gun into Thomas's open wound and repeated his question, "Where can I find your roommate?"

"I don't know! I don't know! I don't know! I don't know where he is. I don't." Thomas started to cough. He thought his body was about to go into shock. Tito started to pat Thomas's pockets. He pulled out Detective Peterson's card and Thomas's wallet. He read the card and then threw it to the ground. He went through Thomas's wallet until he found his license.

Thomas was in so much pain, he paid no attention to anything that was going on. Tito bent over Thomas.

"If I were your friend, I'd be very proud. You are definitely a loyal man. I can respect that, my friend." Tito stood back up and then put the license into his pocket. He started to head toward the door and then turned back to Thomas and fired five shots into his body before he exited the apartment.

11

Derrick and Lisa pulled up outside of her apartment building. There were no lights on inside her unit. It didn't look like anyone was in there.

"See, no one is there. Thomas probably has already been here and left. Let's head to the hotel like he said," Lisa pleaded.

"You might be right." Derrick continued to look around. There was no sign of undercover police. The coast did seem to be clear but Derrick didn't want to be too cautious. "Which apartment is yours?"

"I'm in 202," Lisa said, pointing to it.

"Give me the keys. I'm going to go in and check everything out. If it looks like he has already come and gone, then we're out of here. I want to be sure everything is everything before we leave."

"Fine, but I'm coming with you."

"I don't think that's a smart idea. You should sit tight and wait. What if Thomas is in there and he isn't alone? Then what? We're both caught in the same situation. No, sit here and if I'm not out of there in ten minutes, you get up out of here."

"No," Lisa replied.

"Look, I'm not going to go back and forth with you. Lisa, I need you to sit your ass here. Now give me the keys."

Lisa wasn't used to Derrick being so assertive. She took her house keys off of her key chain and handed them to Derrick. He started to get out of the car when a strange man came out of the building. Lisa grabbed Derrick's arm. "Wait a minute. Someone is coming out."

Derrick turned and looked at the door. "Do you know him? Does he look familiar?"

"No, I've never seen him before. He doesn't live in my building."

The guy walked across the street to a black Tahoe. Once the truck headed down the street, Derrick opened the car door.

"Please be careful, Derrick."

"I'll be aaight." Derrick got out of the car and headed inside the apartment. Derrick's nerves started to kick in. If the alcohol was giving him the courage that always escaped him, the situation at hand had him as sober as could be. He was quickly back to reality. Derrick approached Lisa's door and put the key in.

As he opened the front door, he apprehensively looked around. Everything seemed fine. Derrick closed the door behind him.

"Yo, Tommy, you in here?"

There was no reply. Derrick started to head right back out, until he noticed a chair on the floor. He walked over toward the living room and saw Thomas on the floor. He rushed to him.

"Oh shit! Tommy!" Derrick exclaimed as he collapsed onto the floor next to Thomas. Thomas wasn't responsive. Derrick started shaking him. Thomas came to and let out a loud scream of pure agony.

"Stop trying to move. I'm about to call you an ambulance."

Thomas reached out and grabbed Derrick's hand, stopping him. He put Detective Peterson's card in Derrick's hand.

"What? What is it?" Derrick asked. He looked at what Thomas had placed in his hand. "Is this who did this to you?"

Thomas shook his head.

"He can help you. Call him, he can help," Thomas said. His voice was faint. The front door swung open and Derrick jumped up.

"Lisa, what are you doing here? I told you to wait in the car."

Lisa started to make her way over to Derrick. She still hadn't noticed Thomas lying on the floor, wounded.

"Lisa, go ahead back to the car."

Derrick tried to stop her. It was too late, though. Lisa saw Thomas lying on the floor and rushed over to him.

"Oh my God, baby!" Lisa said as tears started to stream down her face.

Thomas reached up and started to wipe her face clean. "It's okay. I'm going to be aaight. Make sure you take care of him. Now you two get out of here."

Derrick tried to pull Lisa up. "Come on; we need to get out of here."

She pulled away from him and got up.

Derrick realized they needed to get out of there. The scent was starting to get closer to him. Someone was able to find Thomas and then track him down at Lisa's house. For all he knew, the assailant could have been out front waiting for him. But why wait outside? Why not catch them inside the apartment and finish the job, unless they didn't know what Derrick looked like. If that was the case, then it couldn't have been the same person who murdered Jose. Derrick had a lot of questions and thoughts running through his head.

"*Hello!* My boyfriend has been shot. Can you please send an ambulance to—"

Derrick jumped up and grabbed the phone from Lisa. He hung it up. "What are you doing?"

"What the fuck is wrong with you? What do you think I was doing? I was calling an ambulance."

The phone started to ring back.

"Shit, that's probably the damn police. We need to get out of here," Derrick said.

"No, Derrick, things have gone too far. What we need to do is wait for the police to get here and let them handle this. Maybe they can protect us."

The phone stopped ringing.

"No, that's a bad idea. We need to get out of here and think things through. The police will be here soon, so get some things so we can get out of here. You already told them Thomas was shot, so I'm sure they're sending an ambulance also."

"I am not leaving him. I won't do it. You wanted to come over here because if your boy was walking into a trap, you didn't want to leave him hanging. Now you want to pick up and leave him when he needs us the most. I won't do it."

Thomas reached out for Lisa. She knelt back and started to hold his head.

"You have to get out of here," Thomas said before he started coughing.

"No, baby, I won't leave you. I'm not going to do it."

"Come on now; I need you to be strong for the both of us. I'm going to be fine. Go ahead now; get out of here," Thomas reiterated.

Derrick put his hand on Lisa's shoulder. Reluctantly, Lisa gave Thomas a kiss and then got up and went to pack a quick bag.

"Derrick, please be careful. I want you to guard her with your life." Thomas extended his hand out to Derrick. Derrick grabbed a hold of it.

"I promise; I won't let anything happen to her."

Lisa came out of the back room with her bag.

Thomas finished, "Now get out of here and remember, only

Detective Peterson. He is the only one we can trust. No one else; only Detective Peterson."

"I got you."

❈ ❈ ❈

Detective Peterson walked into the crime scene. Two officers greeted him at the door.

"So what do we have here?" Detective Peterson asked.

"We can't call it. It was called in by a woman but when we got here, he was all that was here. He asked for you by name, said he wasn't saying anything to anyone but you. That's why we called you in."

Detective Peterson walked over to the body and saw it was Thomas.

"Shit!"

"Who is he?" one of the officers asked.

"He was a possible witness in my other murder case."

"Not the Benitez case."

"Yeah, that would be the case. He didn't strike me as knowing much about it. I got the impression that he was the link to the missing piece I needed. You said a girl called it in?"

"Yeah, some unidentified woman called in that her boyfriend had been shot and then the call dropped. The owner said the apartment is rented by a Lisa Tolliver."

"You said he asked for me when you got on the scene?"

"Then shortly afterward, he passed. The paramedics weren't able to save him."

"Did he have any ID or anything on him?" Detective Peterson asked.

"No, nothing."

"I want the apartment dusted for prints. I want to know everyone who was in this apartment."

"There was no sign of forced entry. You said he wasn't a major player in your case; you really think your case is linked to this one?"

Lewis walked into the apartment.

"What do we have here?" he asked.

"I'm not sure yet, but I just lost the break in my murder case," Detective Peterson said.

"Who is he?"

"Thomas Sharp. I questioned him earlier today and didn't get the sense that he knew much but he definitely knew something. This just shows me that I wasn't on the wrong track. There is no sign of forced entry, but if you look at his body, you can tell it was a professional hit. No upset girlfriend did this. My guess is one of the Eastside Riderz got a hold of him and tortured him until he gave them the information I was looking for."

Lewis walked over to the body and looked at his wounds. Whoever was there wanted Thomas to feel some pain. If it was Jose's murderer, he would have just put a bullet in Thomas and been on his way. There wouldn't have been anything to question him about, unless Thomas wasn't the one who witnessed the murder and the intruder wasn't the murderer.

"So, the next question is how did Eastside find out about Thomas?"

"My guess would be someone at the newspaper. No one at the station knew about Thomas so it wasn't an internal leak. It had to have come from Thomas's newsroom. Whoever it was knew that Thomas would be here. Guessing from that laptop over there, Thomas worked here often. Who better other than your boss to know your whereabouts? My guess would be his editor is the one who tipped off Eastside."

"Well, let's get their phone records, match the editor up with whoever did this, and then connect the dots that way," Lewis suggested.

"Too much red tape. *Please*, that only gives us who the editor called. It doesn't give us the actual shooter, unless he left behind any DNA or fingerprints that put him in this apartment. If so, then we don't need the editor. Right now, we need to think two steps ahead because we are far behind the murderer and also behind Eastside."

"Well, how did you find out about Thomas?"

Detective Peterson didn't trust anyone inside the department except himself. Though Lewis was working this case with him, he didn't want to give anyone too much information. It wasn't as if he thought Lewis was involved; he always figured you could never be too careful when working a murder.

"That's a dead end street also."

"So we have nothing, really? If we don't find something, Omar is going to find out everything and then there is no justice. The murderer will face the same fate as this guy right here and Omar will go back to business as usual."

"Then we have to figure out a way to stop him. If not, then you're right. Omar is already ahead of us. He found Thomas and whatever he knew, he now knows. What we need to do is figure out what it is that Thomas knew and go from there."

Detective Peterson walked out of the door.

12

Detective Peterson couldn't shake Thomas's murder. He had led Omar straight to Thomas. He should've been more careful. He should've taken more precautions. Whoever killed Thomas had taken his wallet. There was no way someone like Thomas would go anywhere without his credentials. The minute he left the newsroom earlier, that's the first thing he did was get Thomas's home address so he could pay his roommate a visit later on that evening. Why not now?

Detective Peterson thought he might even get lucky and catch the killer at their home, be able to close the books on Thomas's murder, and be a step closer to doing the same with Jose's. He even might be able to build a case against Omar. Life in prison might be just the bargaining tool he could use against Thomas's killer to give up Omar.

Detective Peterson pulled up in front of Thomas's building. The scene on Minnesota Avenue was far from quiet. The everyday drug traffic was evident. The corner boys were in their positions, ready for the possible sales. He wasn't sure what he was walking into. Detective Peterson approached the entrance to the building cautiously. Once he was inside, he drew his gun. He was dealing with a professional so there was no way he was going to be caught off-guard.

Detective Peterson approached Thomas's front door. He could

see the lock had been picked. The door was slightly cracked. Detective Peterson feared he might be too late. He opened the front door and surveyed the apartment. It was totally dark inside. He stumbled over furniture and more, but it appeared he was the only one in the apartment. He briefly checked each room to make sure. There was no sign of anyone else.

The coast was clear. Detective Peterson was alone. Feeling a little more comfortable, Detective Peterson put his gun away. He went back into the living room and turned on the lights. He started to look around the apartment for any clues. He needed to find Thomas's roommate and fast. He looked for anything in the apartment that would put him closer to finding him.

For this to be a bachelors' apartment, it was mighty clean. There was hardly anything left lying around. There was mail lying on the table in the dining room. Detective Peterson went through it.

Derrick Anderson, Detective Peterson thought. Now he finally had a name for the person he was looking for. He took out his cell phone and placed a call.

"Hey, this is Peterson. Is Lewis in the office?" He paused. "Okay, I'm going to be out in the field. If the lab report comes back on the Sharp homicide, send it to my phone or, if Lewis comes in, tell him to call me on my cell."

Detective Peterson hung up the phone. He continued to look through the apartment. He went into Thomas's bedroom. There wasn't much in there. He found a picture of him and Lisa together. He put the picture in his pocket. As he started to leave the room, he heard a noise coming from the other room.

Detective Peterson drew his gun. Before he had only done a general check of each room. He didn't thoroughly check every room. He opened the door to Derrick's bedroom. Cautiously, he opened the closet door. Again, there was nothing. No one was inside the room. Maybe he was tripping. Then right before he turned around, someone hit him on the back of his head. The blow knocked Detective Peterson totally out. Tito bent over and checked his pockets. He pulled out his wallet and saw his badge. Tito threw the wallet down on the floor next to Detective Peterson.

He had no need for it and there was definitely no need to kill a detective. He took what he came there to get and left the apartment. Tito got to his car and called Omar to have him meet him. He needed to bring him up to speed on the situation.

✠✠✠

Tito pulled up to Burger King in Eastover. He wanted to be able to see any and everything that approached. He thought it seemed as if a car had been following him along the ride but the car had turned off a little ways back. Tito noticed Omar's car pulling up. He got out of the car. Omar's car parked next to Tito's. Tito opened the door and Omar exited the car.

"Let's go for a walk," Tito said.

"For what?"

"I'd feel more comfortable. Too much has been going on tonight. Someone was following me."

"La policía?"

"I'm not sure," Tito replied.

Omar gestured to Tito to lead the way. Once they started to walk off, Omar's driver got out of the car and surveyed the parking lot.

"So, what's the urgency, my friend?"

"The reporter was a dead end, but I found out he has a roommate. He might have been the true target of the police."

"Okay, so we find the friend."

"That might be a little harder than the reporter. There is nothing on him. My source didn't even know the reporter had a roommate. All he knew about was the girl."

"So we go through the girlfriend. If the reporter spent as much time as he did with the girlfriend, there's no way she doesn't know about the roommate. We find her and she'll give us the roommate. She shouldn't be hard to find; especially with the death of the reporter. If there's one place she'll be, it's the funeral. Actually, both of them should be."

"I thought of that, but I don't know what either of them look like. Plus, do we really have that kind of time? His funeral won't take place for several days. We need to end this now." Tito paused, deep in thought. "There was a picture of the girl at the reporter's apartment but, before I could get it, the cop showed up."

"What cop?" Omar asked.

"That's the other problem. The detective assigned to Jose's case was at the reporter's apartment. My guess is that he rushed over there after he found out about the murder. But he had no back up. He came solo."

"He must know about the roommate, or he could've simply been checking into the history of the victim. That's basic police work. Did he see you?"

"No, I caught him by surprise and knocked him out. He didn't get a look at me. I figured we didn't need the added heat so I left him there."

Omar nodded. "There's no need trying to see if we can flip him. He definitely isn't on our payroll and his ambition is keeping this case close to him. He showed up by himself because he felt like he couldn't trust anyone with the information, out of fear that it would make its way back to us. There's no sense in trying to bribe a man like that. For right now, don't worry about the detective. He has nothing that can tie us to the reporter's murder and we'll keep it that way. Where is the gun?"

"I haven't had time to dispose of it yet, but the minute we finish here, I'll be throwing it over the Woodrow Wilson Bridge. They'll never find it and even if they do, there will be no trace back to any of us."

Tito noticed a car that resembled the one that was following him earlier making its way toward the both of them. He didn't hear a word that came out of Omar's mouth. The closer the car got to them, the more it started to speed up. Tito quickly grabbed Omar and threw him to the ground in front of an abandoned car. The men within the oncoming car opened fired against them. Tito also took cover and started to fire back.

Two men, both with masks on, continued to fire at Omar and Tito. Neither of them must have noticed Omar's driver. He returned fire back at the car, catching their attention. One of the men returned fire with his automatic weapon and struck Omar's driver. He went down from the gunshots. Just as he did, Tito started to fire back at the car. The glass on the front windshield was hit.

"La pistol!" Omar yelled.

Tito threw his spare gun at Omar. Omar and Tito both returned fire on the car. The shots from both parties rung out. Tito wasn't sure how much longer they'd be able to make it. He was running out of bullets and Omar wouldn't be too far behind. Tito fired two more shots, this time hitting the gunman in the back seat, and shattering the front windshield.

The driver of the car panicked and stepped on the gas. As they were driving away, the other passenger continued to fire on Omar and Tito. Omar realized that there was no way the police weren't called. There were too many people around the area and driving on Indian Head Highway not to have called the police.

"We need to get out of here," Omar said.

Tito went over to Omar's driver to check to see if he was alive. He still had a pulse. Tito picked him up to put him in the car. Omar already had the car started. Tito put the driver in the car, closed the door, and then got in his car to follow Omar. They headed for Interstate 495 to head into Virginia. They needed to dump both cars, and fast. They pulled up to a construction site in Alexandria, Virginia, not too far from the highway. Omar called for someone to come pick them up.

"That was the same car that I thought was following me earlier. I knew something wasn't right."

"When did you first notice it? Was it on you when you left the reporter's apartment?"

"No, definitely not then. I went to one of the drop spots and placed the call to you to meet me. After I left there was when I noticed the car, but then it turned off so I thought I was over-reacting."

"They sat on the drop spot waiting on you."

"Why not take me out when I went in, or when I came out then? Why follow me?" Tito asked.

"They hoped you'd lead them to me."

"Shit! We need to get you into hiding. If they were after you, then we know why they went after Jose."

"They're trying to move in on us. They went after Jose to hurt me. I've always been their target. Now that we know what they want, we give it to them."

"What?" Tito questioned. "Because of my carelessness, they almost succeeded and got you today. There is no way I'll allow you to continue to walk around unprotected for them to get another shot at you."

"That's not what we're going to give them. We're going to give them the war they want. First things first, we need to torch this car. Then, the minute we get back in the city, I want to know where Carlos and his little friend are at all times."

"I'm on it."

"Whoever that was, they definitely weren't professional. That wasn't who killed Jose, but they are all linked together."

"What about the reporter's roommate?"

"I still want you to work that. When I need Carlos and his friend taken care of, then we'll come off the roommate, but for right now, we track Trinidad and find the roommate. None of them get a pass. I want everyone involved. I don't care how big or how small; none of them are walking away from this. All of them will meet the same fate."

13

L isa sat on the end of the bed, worried sick about Thomas. She didn't want to leave him. She wanted to stay right there and wait for the ambulance to arrive. Thomas needed her and she had left. She tried to fight back the tears. However, that was a battle she wasn't winning.

Derrick sat in a chair opposite Lisa in the motel room, staring at the wall. A lot had happened and nothing made any sense. He didn't understand why anyone would go after Thomas. He didn't know anything. He hadn't seen anything. Derrick had. So he could only imagine what the killer would do to him once he finally caught him. But how was he that good, that he was able to find Derrick at Lisa's? Why would he even go to Lisa's for Derrick? Nothing made sense to him, but without the answers, how was he going to save his own life, or Lisa's for that matter?

Derrick tried to replay everything in his mind. But the more he thought, the more confused he made himself. The plan was for them to meet up at the bowling alley and then they were going to go from there. He had to be missing something. They didn't really talk about much so how could so much happen? Then Derrick remembered, Thomas did mention that he was going to check with Lisa to see if it was okay if he stayed at her house to let everything in the streets cool off.

Thomas jumped up out of his seat and caught Lisa by surprise.

He rushed over to her. "When did Thomas ask you if I could crash at your house?"

"I don't know," Lisa replied.

"Come on; I need you to concentrate and really think about it."

"My boyfriend might be fucking dead and you want me to sit here and think about when he asked me if you could stay at my house. You can't be serious."

It was evident that Lisa was on edge. The uncertainty of Thomas's status was really getting to her. Derrick didn't want to seem insensitive.

"I apologize. I didn't mean it like that. I'm worried about Thomas, too. That's why I'm trying to get to the bottom of all this. Somehow, whoever shot him knew to go to your house. Now you said the police were following y'all earlier. I'm pretty sure they ran your tags and probably would've gone to your house to see if either you'd come home to question you, or to see if you had brought Thomas back to your house. Either way, they aren't going to try to kill Thomas."

"What's your point?" Lisa asked, confused.

"My point is someone else had to have known that Thomas would be at your house or, better yet, thought I was already there."

"Why would anyone care if you were there or not?"

"Because I'm the one everyone is looking for," Derrick replied. Lisa didn't know how to react. She was caught off-guard by everything. She sat there and stared at Derrick. Derrick continued by saying, "Thomas was trying to protect me."

"So you mean to tell me, all of this was because of you? EVERYTHING!"

"Yes. This morning, when I was at the bus stop, I saw Jose Benitez murdered and the guy tried to kill me but I was able to get away. I didn't know what to do. I didn't know where to turn and I was starting to panic so instead, I called Thomas. I figured he'd know what to do."

Lisa got hysterical and started to violently swing on Derrick.

"It's all your fault! This is all your fault!" Lisa yelled as she continued trying to hit Derrick. Derrick grabbed a hold of her and tried to hug her. Lisa was upset and looking for anyone to blame for what had happened to Thomas.

"We're going to get through this. I promise, we will. I promised Thomas that I wouldn't let anything happen to you and I meant it."

Lisa pushed Derrick off of her. "How, Derrick? How the hell are we going to do that? Thomas is probably dead right now because of all of this, but yet, we're magically going to come out alright."

"That's why I need you to really think back to when Thomas asked you if I could stay with you. Who was around you? Who might have heard you? Think really hard."

"No one was around me. I was at work."

"Are you sure?"

"Yes, I was in my office when he called me. No one was in there with me."

"Shit! Then how the hell would anyone know to go to your house?"

Derrick stood there, trying to think of what was in front of him that he wasn't seeing. There had to be something he was missing. Everything started and ended with him. Regardless of who was doing the searching, it was him they were searching for. Why would anyone look for him at his best friend's girlfriend's house?

"Wait a minute," Lisa said.

"What's up?"

"Thomas was at work also when he asked me, but he had to get off the phone to go into a last-minute meeting."

"Okay," Derrick said, confused.

"The only person that would've come to look for him to tell him about a meeting would've been George."

"Who is George?"

"Thomas's editor. It had to have been him. He's the only one it could've been; plus, he knows that Thomas works from my house at times. I wouldn't even be surprised if he didn't hear anything Thomas said to me at all. He probably didn't know anything, but knew that more-than-likely, Thomas would be at my house."

"Let's assume that's true; it still doesn't explain how anyone would know about Thomas, or even to ask George about Thomas unless..." Derrick paused.

"Unless what?" Lisa asked.

Derrick pulled Detective Peterson's card out of his pocket and showed it to Lisa. "Unless the police questioned Thomas at his job and George heard that conversation. This is what Thomas gave me when we found him. At first, I thought he was trying to tell me who shot him. But he told me to only talk to him. When did he have time to talk to him, unless that was his meeting?"

"So the police go there to talk to Thomas, to find out what he knows, and George hears the whole conversation and then tells the killer how to find you?"

"No, not the killer. He told Omar Benitez. Everyone keeps saying how powerful he is. So if he has the police on the payroll, why wouldn't he have reporters also? The price for information on his nephew's murder has to be high. George finds out that Thomas knows something, so he tells Omar. Omar pays Thomas a visit and Thomas doesn't give me up so Omar shoots Thomas."

"So why this detective, then? If it was Omar, then Thomas knows just as much as anyone that the police would be the last people to trust."

"I don't know. He must've trusted him because he told me to talk to him and only him. The only way we'll find out is to call him."

"Are you sure?"

"No, I'm not. But what choice do we have?" Derrick picked up the phone.

"Don't call from the hotel phone. Call from your cell phone number and block the call."

"It's the police; they can figure out what my cell phone number is."

"Then don't block your number, but don't call from the hotel phone or they will know where we are. I realize that you feel as though we can trust this guy, but for all we know, this is the person who shot Thomas and you misunderstood why he was giving you his card. Maybe he meant he is the only one who had anything to do with it. I don't know. Just don't call from the hotel phone."

Derrick hung up the hotel phone and took out his cell phone to make the call instead.

✠✠✠

The phone continued to ring as Detective Peterson lay unconscious on the floor. The repeated sound of the ringer over and over again snapped him from his daze. He rolled over and sat up. Everything still seemed hazy. It was all a blur.

Detective Peterson tried to remember what had happened. He remembered checking on a noise but seeing no one was there. Someone must have been in there with him. His phone started to ring again.

"Peterson," he said as he answered the phone.

"Where are you? The desk clerk said you were trying to reach me," Lewis said.

"Yeah, that was earlier; don't worry about it."

"Where are you?"

"I was checking up on a lead. Stay at the station; I'm about to head to you now."

"Meet me at 2806 Martin Luther King, Jr. Avenue in Southeast."

"Why; what's going on there?"

"We have another body in the alley behind the Pepco building."

"Any info on it?"

"No, nothing yet. I was just told we needed to get over there."

"I'm about ten minutes away."

Detective Peterson tried to stand up. He was still very woozy. He bent over, trying to collect himself before he did more harm to himself than good. His phone started to ring again.

"Peterson." There was no reply. "Hello, Peterson," he said again. Still, there was no reply. He moved the phone away from him to look at the number. He didn't recognize it. "Who is this?"

"You spoke to my friend earlier today," Derrick replied.

"What friend might that be?"

"If you don't know, then I don't know. Maybe I have the wrong number."

"I'm pretty sure you don't or you wouldn't have called. I only said my name three times and you reply back with I spoke with your friend today? Obviously your friend said he spoke with me or you wouldn't have said that, so tell me what friend."

"Thomas."

"Is this Mr. Anderson?"

Derrick was caught off-guard by Detective Peterson's question. He knew his name. He didn't know how to reply. He still had no idea what Detective Peterson's motives were.

"My name doesn't matter. What matters is why you are looking for me?"

"Mr. Anderson, you know why I'm looking for you. You already know what information I'm looking for."

"No, I don't. I don't know shit. Actually, I take that back, I do know some things. I can't trust the police. That is what I know. Talking to y'all is no better than talking to a stranger on the street."

"True, very true, but not all of us. There are some cops who take their jobs very seriously."

"And how am I supposed to know that you're one of them?' Derrick asked.

"If you didn't, then you wouldn't even be calling me. By you calling, you must know that something is different. You have to trust something or you wouldn't have even made the call."

"Right now, I don't trust shit."

"Then allow me to build that trust. I can't protect you if you don't let me."

"You mean like you protected my friend!"

"He wouldn't allow me to protect him. I'm sorry about your friend's death. I really am, but my hands were tied. He didn't want my help. He wouldn't let me help. He thought the same as you, that I couldn't protect you. He didn't give me the chance."

"What do you mean, death? What are you talking about?"

"You didn't know? I figured you knew he was shot. I'm sorry, but Thomas died earlier."

Tears started to roll down Derrick's face. A part of him thought Thomas would pull through. He was talking to him and everything. He was too strong to die.

Detective Peterson continued, "Please, Mr. Anderson, allow me to help you."

"Omar Benitez is too powerful. Thomas didn't trust you fully and neither will I, but I will help you find whoever killed Omar's nephew. If the killer is caught, then no one will want me."

Detective Peterson didn't want to agree but if he didn't, then Derrick didn't have to give him anything and could end up dead also. Then Detective Peterson wouldn't have anything.

"How can you help me find the killer?"

"I'm the only person who knows what he looks like. I saw the whole thing this morning when I was waiting for the bus. He didn't see me until after it was all over."

"Whoever killed Jose had to be a player in the game. I want you to look at some pictures of hitters for different crews in the street."

"And where do you expect me to do this? I told you, I don't trust you. I'm not coming to a police station. Benitez and his crew are looking for me now. I'll be damned if I come to the police station, out of all places, and make it easy for him to find me. It won't be long before I'm like Thomas. No, I'll pass."

"Omar doesn't know about you, unless he is the one who had his nephew killed. I told no one about Thomas or you; I didn't want that information leaked. I'm working this case by myself for a reason."

"Omar is the one who shot Thomas. Thomas's editor must have told him after you left his office earlier today. They weren't looking for Thomas; they were looking for me and Thomas wouldn't give me up."

"You witnessed all of this?"

"No, not that; only Omar's nephew's murder. I put the pieces together. You aren't the only one who can solve things."

"You name the place and time and I'm there."

Derrick thought long and hard. It was already dark outside so that night was out of the question. He was going to make sure they met in the daytime at a crowded location.

"We can meet tomorrow at one p.m. at Iverson Mall. Park in front of the Bojangles and we'll go from there."

"That sounds like a plan," Detective Peterson agreed.

"And you need to come by yourself. If I see anything fishy, I'm out of there and you will never hear from me again."

"I understand completely."

"Good, it's always good to be on the same page. I'm glad we are," Derrick said and then hung up the phone.

14

Carlos walked into the apartment. As he was closing the door, Tony was there to greet him. Tony grabbed Carlos by his collar and slammed him into the door, knocking it shut.

"What the fuck were you thinking?" Tony asked.

"Get off of me," Carlos replied, trying to break free.

Tony outweighed him by nearly fifty pounds. There was no way he was breaking free. He continued to struggle.

"You are about to fuck everything up. I said we needed to be smart about this shit and you go and do this. What are you trying to do, get us all killed?"

"You're the one who said we needed to step things up. I just put some actions behind your words; not mine."

"No, I said put our guy on him; that's what I said. I didn't say do it your damn self."

Frustrated by everything, Tony let Carlos go and walked off. Carlos started to straighten out his clothes. Though Carlos would never admit it in front of anyone, he understood who ran the show. Out of respect for their friendship and partnership, Tony never enforced his power in front of others, but when they were alone, he'd quickly get Carlos in line if needed.

"So what the hell happened?" Tony asked.

"The plan was to set up on Tito. Then he went to meet Omar and we figured why not take both out at one time."

"So what happened then?"

"Tito, this nigga's tougher with the pistol than I thought. Mike got hit."

"Shit, I knew this was going to happen."

"What?"

"You fucking up and doing too much. Now we're the ones who need to lay low. If he didn't know we were behind everything, he damn sure does now."

"You are a worrier, my friend. We had masks on and we used a stolen car. Nothing can be traced back to us."

"Nothing can be traced back, huh? What about the fact that now you and I aren't the only two who know what we are up to? What about Mike? I'm sure Tito knows he hit someone and miraculously Mike has gunshot wounds. How stupid do you think people really are? I keep telling you; we have to be smart about this shit."

"I really think you're making too much out of this. You are giving them way too much credit. Keep in mind; I was close at hitting their head. Their eyes are wide awake now. No one has ever tried to go at them. We almost got them."

"Do you even hear what you're saying? Maybe you need to pay attention to yourself. One, you think we are the first to go at them? Yeah, right! Second, they almost got their head hit. You think they aren't going to beat these streets to find out by whom? They aren't going to tuck their skirts and run; no, they are going to strap up them boots and go to war. A war we can't win head to head, might I add. That was the whole purpose of the planned SURPRISE attempt," Tony said and then hit Carlos on the back of the head.

"Well, there's nothing we can do about what's already done. Right now, the only thing we can do is go from here. What's done is done, so what's the plan?"

"If we go into hiding, then we'll look like bitches when Omar comes knocking so that's not an option. Even if we did get at him, why would anyone take us serious after finding out we went into hiding during war? I damn sure wouldn't."

"Fuck that; I hide from no man. I die on my feet before I ever live on my knees; please believe that!" Carlos shot back.

"Well, you keep the dumb shit you've been doing up and you'll definitely die on your feet. Where is Mike?"

"He went to see the doctor?"

Tony started shaking his head. *The doctor* was a licensed physician who traded drugs for services. The only problem was that every drug dealer went to him. He was hired help and everyone knew about him. He had no loyalties to anyone but definitely wouldn't cross Omar for anyone either. The minute Omar started asking questions, the doctor would have all the answers for him.

"Shit, I would've had him go to an actual hospital. At least, make it somewhat hard for this nigga, damn! Find out if Mike is still there and, if so, tell him that you'll send someone to pick him up. Then this nigga needs to be floating in someone's river, him and whoever else was with you. I want both of them niggas gone before the morning."

"What!" Carlos replied.

"We don't need any loose edges right now. Both of them niggas are the only links to us. If Tito or Omar gets their hands on either one of them, please believe both of them are giving us up without hesitation. They've got to!"

"Okay, I'm on it. What about Omar and Tito?"

"I'll take care of both of them. You make sure you do what I asked you to do," Tony replied.

"Stop talking to me like I'm some retard or something shit!"

"Then stop doing retarded shit. Now get out of your feelings and do what I need you to do and be careful. You need to keep both eyes open at all times."

"I got this," Carlos replied.

"Carlos, I'm serious. This ain't no game. Tito plays for keeps and he always comes out on the winning side. I get on you a lot but I'm not trying to attend your funeral and I'm damn sure not trying to be playing in the plot next to you no time soon. Be careful out there. Don't take no chances. If something don't look right, don't sit there and wait. Start shooting first and then ask questions later. Don't risk shit out there, you hear me?"

"Oh, no doubt! You don't have to worry about that. You know me."

✠✠✠

Detective Peterson pulled up to the crime scene. The alley was roped off in police tape. Detective Peterson approached Lewis.

"So what do we have here?"

"Gunshot wound to an unknown number one male."

"Any witness?"

"No, nothing here but the medical examiner said she thinks the body was moved. He wasn't killed here. This is the dumping ground."

"Any ideas?"

"Well, there was a report of a shootout in Eastover but by the time PG police got on the scene, there was nothing or anyone there. It was some kind of argument at Burger King or something. The details are still unclear but my guess would be we have one of the participants."

Detective Peterson removed the sheet off of the body. Right away he recognized who it was.

"You don't know who this is?" Detective Peterson asked.

"No, should I?"

"I'd hope so since we saw him earlier. This is Omar's driver."

"What! First Jose, now Omar's driver? There is no way this is a coincidence."

"Exactly, and if I were a gambling man, I'd surely have my money on the fact that he wasn't the target either. Someone tried to hit Omar and missed."

"Who would be stupid enough to do something like that? I don't have anyone in their right mind trying to go heads up with Eastside. You're usually right on point with your hunches but I don't know about this one."

"I pray that I'm wrong; I really do. If there is one thing I know about Omar, it's the fact that he never goes anywhere without his driver. The driver stays glued to Omar's ass. If he got hit, Omar was with him when it happened."

"Let's say that's the case. Who has balls enough to go at Omar head to head out here?'

"It's like you said, I don't have anyone doing that either. That's like a suicide mission. But whoever it is, they are talking. Anyone who comes this close, it's going to get out there. They are going to want the respect that comes with going at Omar and succeeding to a certain degree."

"So what's the plan? Right now we have pretty much nothing but speculation for everything."

"Sometimes speculation is all you can go off of; that and assumptions and that's exactly what we are going to do. If someone is after Omar, then it won't be long before they try to hit him again. At this point, that's the only move they have, except going in hiding and there isn't anywhere you can hide in this city without Omar finding you. The only move they have is to finish the job before Omar finishes them. So, for now, we sit on Omar and allow him to lead us to whoever is after him; then we put the pieces to the puzzle together from there."

"So now we're in the business of saving him also?"

'No, we're in the business of doing our jobs, no more and no less. Now, if that's too much for you, let me know and I can go about this alone."

"Calm down, Pete; it's really not that serious. You hate Benitez as much as I do and I'm thinking if someone kills him, then he'd be doing us all a favor. Then Omar would be gone and we could lock up the murder and put down Jose's murder. It seemed like a win-win to me."

"Well, how do you plan on catching whoever in the act, if you aren't sitting on Omar? Keep in mind; we don't even know who is trying to kill him. We don't even know if anyone is trying to kill him. Right now, we are merely trying to get some of the answers to these looming questions. We have to connect the dots."

"I'm with you. So while I'm sitting on Omar, what are you going to do?"

"What I always do, I'm going to try to shake some trees and see what falls out. Remember, if anything pops off, call me. Please don't try to be no hero. Now go home and get some sleep. We're going to have a long day ahead of us tomorrow."

"Hopefully nothing pops off tonight," Lewis replied.

"I'm already two steps ahead of you. I'm going to send a couple of patrol cars around Congress Heights to sit and keep things calm tonight. I don't have Omar hitting back tonight. If anything, he'll sit back and try to plan everything out just right."

15

Derrick didn't sleep well at all. His mind continued to stay on everything that was going on. For the most part, Lisa lay in bed. The reality of Thomas's death really finally started to hit her. She was in total disbelief about all that had transpired in one day. She felt as though this whole nightmare was nothing more than a dream. But once she woke up that morning, the reality of everything smacked her in the face yet again.

They were out of the hotel room early. Derrick wanted to make sure they were the first at the mall. There was no way he was going to allow them to walk into a trap. He thought Detective Peterson could be trusted, but he also realized that everyone made mistakes.

"How long do we have to sit here?" Lisa questioned.

"If you would've stayed in the hotel room like I said, then you would've been fine."

"Well, I didn't. I'm here so deal with it. I told you, I wasn't staying in the damn room."

"Then please, stop complaining."

"No! We shouldn't even be here. For all we know, this detective has us walking right into a trap. We should just get out of D.C."

"And then what?"

"I don't know. Anything is better than being in this parking lot like sitting ducks."

"We both have family here. Running does us no good. I've already told you, if you want to go, cool. I certainly would under- stand and actually would support the whole idea. It probably would be much safer for you. I'd feel a little more at-ease."

"And where would I go?"

"Lisa, aren't you the one who wants to run?"

"Yeah, but what does that have to do with anything?"

Derrick didn't even respond. He shook his head. An oncoming car caught Derrick's attention. It was a black Chevy Impala. It looked like the typical unmarked police car. Derrick had no clue what Detective Peterson looked like, so he wasn't too sure. Derrick had given Detective Peterson strict instructions.

Lisa continued, "Plus, I said, why don't we get out of here? That means the both of us. I also promised Thomas that I would make sure nothing happened to you."

Derrick continued to watch the car. At first it went to the Bojangles side of the parking lot, but then it drove off and went around the parking lot. The car passed right in front of them. Derrick struggled to see inside the car.

"Derrick, are you paying any attention to me?" Lisa asked as she noticed Derrick's attention was somewhere else.

"Huh? What did you say?"

Lisa started to look around. She didn't see anything.

"What is it, Derrick? What the hell is going on?"

"Nothing; what were you saying again?"

"Derrick, what?" Lisa asked again.

"Nothing, I don't want you freaking out over something that might be nothing at all, so let it go."

"I wish that you'd stop treating me like I'm a damn child, or something. Please, tell me what the hell is *it*?"

"Do you see that car right there? He's been circling the parking lot. He first came in and went over to Bojangles and then drove over there; now he's parked there."

"What's your point? Do you think that's him?"

"No, I don't think so. I expected him to arrive early and check out the scene also, but why park over there? If it was him, he would've stayed parked in front of Bojangles."

"So who is that?"

"I don't know. I told you, it might not be anyone. We're at a mall; maybe he's meeting someone. I don't know. Plus, look at the car. At first, I thought it was an unmarked car but can you have tinted windows on an unmarked car?"

"Then why hasn't he gotten out of the car? Why don't you call the guy and see where he is? If he says that he's here, then we know that's him. If he isn't here, then that's fine also. But at least we aren't sitting here all paranoid and shit."

"Who is paranoid?"

"I am, damn it. This shit is working my nerves."

Derrick took out his phone and dialed Detective Peterson's number.

"This is Peterson," Detective Peterson said, answering the call.

"Maybe we should just call this whole thing off. I'm really not feeling it."

"Mr. Anderson, everything is going to work itself out. I told you; allow me to build your trust in me."

"Yeah, I heard all of that but I'm not feeling it. I did a lot of thinking last night and if I stay hidden, I'll be just fine. I can relocate."

"Then your friend's death would've been all for nothing. You said that he was killed because he wouldn't tell them where you were. Now I would think you would want to see the same men who killed your friend brought to justice. See this thing through first and then, if you want to relocate, fine. But please, see this thing through."

"How far are you from the meeting spot?" Derrick asked.

"I'm on my way there now. I should be pulling up in the next ten minutes."

"Okay."

"Will you be there when I get there?" Detective Peterson asked.

"Yeah, just hurry up. I want to get this over with," Derrick replied before hanging up the phone. He turned to Lisa, "Yeah, that's not him. He said he's about ten minutes away. But he still hasn't gotten out of the car yet. He's sitting there for something. What, that I don't know, but we are going to find out. Look, I'm going to go inside the mall. That way, I can get a better look."

"Derrick, I don't think that's a smart idea. If you really trust this cop, then let's wait until he gets here, or let's get out of here now."

"Lisa, it's probably nothing. I want to get a look inside the car. I didn't say that I was going to get into the car. I'm going to walk past it. Something isn't right. If you look at it, he's in perfect position to see Bojangles just like we are. Maybe I'm getting paranoid like you, maybe I'm not, but what I will do is make sure nothing happens to either of us. Now if something goes down, I want you to get out of here. Head back to the hotel and if I'm not back there by tonight, then you get your ass out of D.C. and don't look back."

"Derrick, stop talking like that. I'm not going to leave you. We're in this together."

"Lisa, please, don't fight me on this."

"Derrick, I will not leave you, and I'm coming with you."

"No, I need you to keep an eye out for the detective. He might come while I'm inside. Stop trying to fight me on every fucking thing. Just sit here; I'll be back."

Derrick opened the car door and started walking toward the

mall entrance. He approached the suspicious car and tried to get a good view inside. The driver's face was one that he'd never forget. It was the same face he had seen the day before that had started this whole ordeal. It was the face of the killer. Derrick started to pick his pace up and walked faster toward the entrance.

Derrick's hopes that maybe the killer didn't notice him walking by were quickly shattered. When he turned around to get a glimpse, he saw the killer getting out of his car and heading toward the mall entrance as well. Once Derrick got inside, he started to run deeper into the mall. It would only be a matter of time before the killer was inside, but Derrick realized that the killer wouldn't risk killing him in front of witnesses.

Derrick could make it to the exit on the other end of the mall toward the back parking lot. Once he was there, he could head down the ramp toward the street and figure out the rest once there. As he made his way toward the back exit, he changed his mind and went into a barbershop. He looked into the mall from the window and tried to see if he saw the killer.

If there was ever a time to approach the killer, now was that time. Derrick noticed him over by the food court area. The killer was looking around to see if he spotted Derrick. Derrick took out his cell phone and called Lisa.

"Derrick, that guy followed you into the mall. You need to get out of there," Lisa said once she answered the phone.

"I saw him. It's the same guy who killed Jose yesterday. You were right about Detective Peterson. He must've tipped the killer off. Look, I want you to drive to the other side of the street and I'm going to come out of Forman Mills."

"I'm on my way over there now. Derrick, please be careful."

"I'll be fine. He isn't going to do anything in here and risk having more witnesses. You just make sure you're careful. Get your butt over there now, and keep the car running."

As Derrick hung up the phone, he started walking toward the killer. He zoomed in on his face with his camera phone and took his picture. He hadn't worked out what he was going to do or how he would even get himself out of this situation. He was doing everything strictly off impulse. He could run all day long, but running no longer seemed like an option. He figured, why not confront the killer?

As he started to get closer to him, the killer noticed Derrick. He started to make his way to him. In case Derrick was planning on running, he could be close on the chase.

"You've got some balls, I see," the killer said as they approached one another.

"I wouldn't say all of that. I realize that you're a smart man and not dumb enough to do anything in here with all these witnesses around."

The killer surveyed his surroundings. No one was paying them any attention, but to be early in the afternoon, the mall was pretty packed. The minute shots fired, everyone would be trying to see where they came from and who fired them. That was just the nosey habit of most people.

"Look, whatever is going on between you and Benitez, I have nothing to do with it. You don't have to worry about me going to the police. So why don't you turn around and walk out of the mall; I'll do the same thing and you can forget about me. I'll even make sure to get myself out of town. You won't ever hear or see from me again."

"Let's go outside and talk about this a little more," the killer replied.

Derrick knew better than to do that. "Naw, I'm good. We can discuss everything right here and once we agree, you go your way and I'll go mine."

The killer exposed his pistol on his hip. He didn't want to pull it out in front of everyone, but wanted Derrick to be aware that he was carrying.

"That's not going to work; now let's go."

"What are you going to do; shoot me in front of everyone?"

"If I have to, I will. Everyone will be too busy running or ducking in panic; no one will even pay attention to your ass lying on the floor until I'm gone like the wind. Now let's go."

The killer drew his pistol and came in closer to Derrick. He stuck it in Derrick's ribcage so that no one could visibly see it. They would have to concentrate on the two of them to know something was wrong.

The killer said, "Now, let's go."

Derrick started to walk along with him toward the back exit. If they made it into the back parking lot, his chances of surviving were slim to none. Derrick quickly jabbed his elbow into the killer's ribcage, catching him off-guard and almost knocking the breath out of him. As the killer was staggering from the blow, Derrick swung a furious left hook that connected to the killer's chin. He instantaneously went down from the punch.

As the killer fell, he dropped his gun. Derrick picked up the gun and ran toward the opposite end of the mall. People started to rush to see what had happened. Some saw Derrick punch the killer and others only saw the reaction to people who saw the whole scene and wanted to see what all the commotion was about. The crowd around made it easier for Derrick to get away. Once the killer got to his feet, he could barely see Derrick.

Derrick ran through Forman Mills and out the front door. Lisa had the car pulled up to the curb and still running. Derrick jumped into the car and Lisa sped off through the parking lot. Derrick's phone started to ring.

"You thought you were going to set my ass up? I shouldn't have trusted you," Derrick said as he picked up the phone.

"What are you talking about? I'm just getting here."

"I bet you are. What, did you want to come to make sure the killer finished the job? Well, I didn't give him a chance. Both of y'all can kiss my ass!"

"Mr. Anderson, what are you talking about? Where did you see the killer? Is he here?" Detective Peterson asked.

Derrick hung up the phone. He didn't know what to believe. He was confused by Detective Peterson.

"I told you not to trust him. I knew he had something to do with Thomas getting killed. I knew it," Lisa said.

"Naw, it wasn't him. He didn't know anything about it."

"Then how did he find us? How would he have known we were meeting the detective today and where? Stop being so naïve, Derrick. He tried to set us up. It was him."

"He didn't know anything a minute ago. He was clueless about everything. There's a certain way a person replies to situations when they know something and it's a totally different way when they have no idea what the hell you're talking about? He was clueless. He knew nothing, but how the killer found out is a question that does concern me. It has to be someone the detective does trust who is leaking the information. But why would the killer be there? Why not Benitez's people, if the information was being leaked by the police?"

"Maybe the killer has a police contact also."

"Yeah, maybe, but I doubt it. I don't know." Derrick took out Detective Peterson's card and then continued. "We're the only ones with information. Let's head to the police station."

"And do what?"

"Sit and wait. Somehow, that's where the missing answers we need are."

16

The scent to Derrick had run dry. Tito had nothing to go off of. He didn't want to just sit and do nothing. So instead, he decided to sit on Carlos or Tony. One of them was behind trying to kill him and Omar. His intuition said it was Carlos. Everything was sloppy. Tony seemed the more organized of the two.

If Tito were a guessing man, he'd say that Tony was the mastermind behind the overall scheme of things and Carlos was the loose cannon leaving the breadcrumbs of clues pointing toward them. That was the reason why Tito decided to set up surveillance on Carlos. Anyone who lacked rational thinking and whose actions couldn't be predicted needed to be monitored. But more than anything, Tito was gambling on Carlos's impulses being his downfall. He hoped the possible mistakes Carlos might make would allow him to eliminate Carlos from any equation.

Tito saw Carlos coming out of the building. He wasn't traveling alone. There was someone else walking with him. If anyone spotted Tito in rival territory, he wouldn't fair well. He couldn't get out of the car and follow them. However, Tito told his understudy, Raul, to do so. No one knew who he was so they could never connect him to Eastside. To them, he'd be just another nigga in the hood.

Carlos kept on with business as usual. He paid no attention to

Tony's warning. He went to each stash spot and checked the nightly intake. Then, after he verified all the funds, he headed to a mom and pop breakfast spot. It looked like a rundown Chinese carryout or something. Once he sat down to eat, Raul called him to let him know where they were. Tito drove to where they were to meet him.

Once Tito's understudy spotted the car, he went over to it and got inside.

"He's in there," Raul said.

"How long has he been in there?"

"Not that long; maybe about ten minutes, if that. What do you want me to do?"

"Is his muscle still with him? How many people are inside?"

"Yeah, his muscle is in there with him but, outside of the people who work there, no one else is in there."

"Perfect; we'll hit him here then."

"Are you sure? What about the old man?"

"I can handle Omar; don't worry about that. You're protected by me. If any flack comes, I'll take the heat on it."

Tito's understudy took out his pistol and cocked it back. "How do you want to play this then?"

"I want you to go inside; more than likely if no one else is in there, that's by design. He probably makes sure the diner is clear while he's there so his muscle is going to get you up and out of there. Put up a little resistance so they come outside with you but not too much so they don't pull out on you."

"I got you."

"I'm going to come in through the back. Once you hear shots fired, his muscle will turn around to come inside and you drop his ass and then get the car." Tito paused for a few seconds. "Give me a minute to get around back first before you go in. I want to make sure he doesn't spot me; the minute he does, the plan is over and we're in a shootout."

Tito got out of the car and made his way behind the diner. The back door was closed. Tito knocked on the door. His knocks went ignored. His plan would go straight downhill if he couldn't get inside the diner. He figured the back door would've been opened since most restaurants leave the doors open so they can take the trash out. Tito knocked again; this time someone came to the door.

"What are you doing coming to the back? Ronald, why didn't you use the front door? I've told you about coming to the back," an old man said, opening the door without even looking to see who was there.

Tito grabbed him and jabbed his pistol in his back. "How many people are in here?"

The old man realized that he didn't open the door for who he initially thought. "Look, young man, we don't carry much money. There is no need in robbing us. There might be thirty dollars in the register, if that. Thirty dollars isn't worth going to jail over."

"Shut up and answer my question and you won't get hurt," Tito replied.

"It's just myself and my cook this early."

"And what about Ronald?"

"He will be coming in soon."

"Okay, let's go," Tito said as he pushed the old man to move forward. They walked into the kitchen and the cook immediately saw them. Tito put his finger over his mouth, letting the cook know not to say a word. Tito waved for the cook to come over to him. The cook did as Tito commanded.

"Do you know who I am?" The cook nodded his head, acknowledging that he did. Tito continued, "Good, then you know what I'm capable of. You and the old man sit over there and don't move or make one sound. If you do as I request, I promise that I will not hurt you. You don't, and you'll end up like the rest of these niggas."

The cook did as asked.

Raul walked into the diner and headed for the counter. Just as Tito had thought, Carlos's man approached Raul.

"Yo, my man, you got to get the fuck out of here. The diner is closed right now."

"What do you mean, the diner is closed? If it's closed, then why is he eating?" Raul asked, pointing at Carlos. "Look, I just want something to eat. I worked a double last night."

"I don't give a shit what you worked. I'm not going to repeat myself; the diner is closed. You need to bounce now, homie. Either you can leave on your own, or I can put you out."

"Over some damn breakfast? It's not even that serious. I'm just trying to get something to eat," Raul said as he turned to make his way toward the door. "Y'all need to do something about the customer service up in this place. Who goes into business not to make money? I mean, you got a damn sign up that says open but yet you closed. Yeah, okay! Talkin' 'bout you going to put me out; I'll beat the shit out of you."

"What the fuck did you say?"

Raul opened the door and walked out. Carlos's man followed outside right behind him.

"I asked you, what did you say? You going to beat whose ass?"

"Look, all I wanted was something to eat. You're the one who started flappin' off at the mouth, talking about putting someone out over some damn breakfast. Really, when did breakfast become that serious?"

"Naw, fuck all that. I'm trying to see this ass-whipping you supposed to be giving me."

While Raul and Carlos's friend were outside arguing, Tito realized that was the perfect time for his surprise attack. Carlos couldn't help but be nosey and continued to peek outside to see what was going on. Tito made his way from out the back and fired two shots into Carlos's arm.

Carlos's friend heard the gunshots and started to make his way back into the diner when Raul shot him in the back. He instantly went down. Raul stood over top of him and fired two more shots into the back of his head, ending his life. Raul turned and ran for the car.

Tito moved in closer to Carlos as he was screaming from the pain.

"I told you, we'd meet again. Now get your ass up and let's go."

"Nigga, fuck you! You going to have to kill my ass. I'm not going a muthafuckin' place."

Tito shot him again, this time in his right shoulder. The pain was getting unbearable for Carlos.

"Now we can do this either your way, or mine. Get your ass up or we'll continue the fun."

"I can't move my fucking arms. How the fuck am I supposed to get up?" Carlos shot back.

"Scoot your ass out that seat and let's go. Last time I checked, you didn't need your arms to walk. Now use those fucking legs and let's go!"

Carlos did as Tito told him to. The two of them walked toward the front door. Raul had the car parked in front of the diner. Carlos looked down and saw his man dead on the ground. Tito pushed Carlos into the car and they drove off.

✠✠✠

Detective Peterson walked into the police station upset. He needed to figure out how the killer knew about his meeting with Derrick. He hadn't told anyone. He didn't trust anyone to tell them. He walked up to the desk sergeant.

"Did I get any calls?" Detective Peterson asked.

"No, nothing," the desk sergeant replied.

Detective Peterson had nothing. He walked off and headed to his desk. He could sense he was close to finally get some answers to the mystery.

Derrick and Lisa sat out front of the police station; waiting. Neither of them knew what Detective Peterson looked like, but this seemed the safest place of all. Plus, whoever was talking to the killer and Omar was here. Maybe that person they would recognize and then they could start to piece more and more together.

Nothing stood out. Everything looked the same. Cops went in and out of the police station. There was nothing out of the ordinary.

"So what are we going to do, sit here and wait?" Lisa asked.

"For right now, yes. The clue we need is here. I don't think that detective is the one who snitched. If he did, why would he tell the same person who killed Jose? That doesn't make any sense. If he was a part of the murder, then why not kill us himself? Why use the killer to do it?"

"Okay, but what are we going to find out by being here?"

"Lisa, I don't know. I'm pulling at anything right now. I don't know what to do! But I'm not going to be a sitting duck, waiting for these muthafuckas to kill me, or you!" Derrick yelled, frustrated.

Lisa didn't know how to reply back. Derrick was trying but she could also see the excitement of everything was finally starting to take its toll on him. Derrick continued to survey the police station.

"Wait a minute; I might have an idea," Lisa said. Derrick looked at her. "The problem is we don't know who this detective is. Call him and tell him you want to meet again. Whoever comes out must be him and then we'll follow him to make sure, and if he goes where we said."

"We don't even know if he's here. What if he's not here, then what? Or what if any detective or officer comes out and we think it's him and follow him?"

"Then we are just wrong but we'll know it's not him if he doesn't go where you tell him to meet you. I mean, anything is worth a shot. Right now, we're sitting here looking for something and we don't even know what it looks like. How does that help? You said you're pulling at straws; I'm trying to make them at least a little longer and easier to grab. Anything is worth a try, Derrick. Plus, what if he did set us up the first time? If he did, he'll do the same again, but this time, we'll be following him so we'll see everything ahead of time."

Derrick thought over Lisa's plan. It actually wasn't that bad. Detective Peterson wasn't an officer in uniform so any uniformed officer that came out of the station after he called obviously wouldn't be him. Plus, now he had a picture of the killer. He didn't need to do a lineup anymore. If everything went as Lisa planned and his suspicions of Detective Peterson were correct, then they'd be able to meet and he could give him the evidence. If he was wrong and Detective Peterson was in on the setup and a part of this whole scheme, then he'd know the next move to make.

"You're right. Anything is worth a try and your plan might actually work."

Detective Peterson's phone started to ring. He immediately

recognized the number. He answered the phone but before he could say a word, Derrick was spitting instructions out to him.

"You say you knew nothing about the hit on me earlier, cool. I'm going to give you another chance to prove your worth. I want you to meet me at the Safeway on Alabama Avenue in ten minutes. If you are there in eleven minutes, I will be gone. And, please don't try anything funny. This time, you won't catch me with my pants down."

Derrick hung up the phone before Detective Peterson could even come back with a reply. Derrick left Detective Peterson with few options. He grabbed his keys off his desk and headed for the door. Derrick noticed him come out of the station and started pointing at him to Lisa.

"Look, right there. That's him," he said.

"I see him. I see him," Lisa replied.

Lisa started up the car. Detective Peterson got into his car and made his way down the street. Lisa pulled the car out and followed behind him.

17

Tony approached the front door cautiously with his gun in hand. Someone was continuously banging on it. Tony opened the door with his gun squarely pointed at the man standing there.

"Will, why the fuck are you knocking on the door like you've lost your damn mind?"

"They've got him!"

"Huh, who has who? What are you talking about?"

"Carlos! Those Eastside niggas got Carlos. They hit him at the diner."

"Shit! How bad is he?"

"We don't know. Paul was out front dead. The owner said Tito came in and took Carlos. He said he was alive when he left but he was shot a couple of times."

"Who do we have on Omar?'

"No one!" Will replied.

"What! What do you mean no one?"

"No one has been able to find him. He went into hiding. What the fuck are we going to do?"

"First of all, you need to calm the hell down. Second, we need to get everyone together."

"And do what?"

"Go hit these muthafuckas right back. We need to find Carlos.

They kept him alive for a reason. If not, then we would've found him and Paul at that diner, both gone. More than likely, they took him back around Congress Heights. That's where we're going."

Will made his way to the front door. He opened it and jumped back as Tito stood there with his gun pointed straight at him. Tony couldn't see Tito; only Will standing there.

"Nigga, I said, let's go. Get everyone together. We don't have a minute to waste."

Will moved to the side and Tito walked inside. His gun was still squarely pointed at Will. Tony immediately drew his pistol.

"Put your shit down!" Tony commanded.

Tito ignored him. He looked at him and cracked a smile. Raul walked in with Carlos. His gun was planted squarely in the back of Carlos's head. Tony quickly reacted and, with his free hand, pulled another pistol from behind his back and pointed it at Raul.

"At this point, I don't give a shit. We'll all die up in this bitch if y'all don't put the fucking guns down!" Tony stated adamantly.

"Are you sure about that?" Omar inquired as he walked into the apartment.

Once Omar was inside, Tony panicked. Instead of keeping one gun on Tito and the other on Raul, he turned his attention off Tito and on to Omar.

That was the mistake Tito was looking for. He fired two shots, both hitting Tony. One hit his left shoulder and the other his left thigh. Tony dropped the pistol that was in his left hand as he fell to the floor.

Omar closed the door behind him. Tito walked Will over to the couch and sat him down. Tony was on the floor, screaming in pain.

"Now, my friend, I told you that I'd be paying you a visit one day soon and, as you see, I'm a man of my word," Omar said. He walked over and grabbed a folded chair that was standing up against the wall. He unfolded it and sat down. Raul and Carlos continued to stand.

"Now, I'm going to ask you some very simple questions and what I expect are some very simple answers. How painless everything is, will depend upon your responses."

Tony tried to pick himself up from off the floor and sit up. He looked around and saw the situation everyone was in. There was no way he was coming out on top. Carlos's face was badly bruised. It was obvious they had beaten Tony's location out of Carlos.

"You might as well get it over with and kill my ass; I'm not telling you nothing," Tony said.

"Have it your way. The hard way it is, my friend," Omar said.

He gave Raul a look and before anyone knew it, Raul had released a single shot into the back of Carlos's head. They'd already gotten all they were going to get out of Carlos. His lifeless body dropped to the floor.

"Man, just tell them what they want to know!" Will yelled.

"Shut your bitch ass up. They're going to kill us regardless. I'm not telling them shit," Tony hissed. He looked at Omar and continued, "You think killing my man is going to scare me. I know the game. That was always the plan. Now, like I said, you might as well get on with it and do whatever it is you're going to do."

Omar looked at Tito. Tito started walking toward Tony as Omar began to laugh.

"Look, your boy already filled in most of the holes for me. I want my nephew's killer and the brains of the whole operation, and then I'm out of your hair. Since you're the one who put out the contract, you can supply me with that."

Tito stepped on the gunshot wound on Tony's left leg. Tony started to scream in pain.

"Is this pain really worth being a hero? Why? You can end this at any moment," Omar said.

Once Tito stopped, Tony reached for his leg and cradled it. Tony wouldn't break. He continued to scream in pain. However, he still wouldn't tell them anything. They didn't have hours on end to torture him. Sooner or later, one of his boys would catch wind to what was going on and make their way into the apartment with guns blazing. All he had to do was hold on a little while longer.

Tito became impatient. He took out a pocket knife, slashed Tony's side twice, and then stabbed him in the gunshot wound to his left thigh. Tony couldn't take it any longer.

"I'm behind it all! I planned the hit!" Tony yelled.

"Bullshit! There's no way you'd know where Jose would be at that time."

Tito jammed his knife back into Tony's gunshot wound again. Tony was losing blood at a rapid rate. The pain was unbearable. Tito pulled the knife out.

"It was me, damn it! Jose's bitch gave him up. She was fucking Carlos and told Carlos everything he wanted to know. How he turned her, I don't know, but she's the one who told us where Jose would be and what time. No one else was in on it. It was only me and Carlos."

Tito looked at Omar to see if believed him and if he should stop, or if he didn't buy it and the torture needed to continue. Omar waved Tito off. Tito wiped his knife off on Tony's leg and then put it away.

"Let's say you're telling the truth. Why Jose?"

"It was never about Jose. It was always about you. You were always the target, but I couldn't get you and leave Jose alive. He'd pick up where you left off. I wanted all of you Eastside bitches gone, but with you and Jose gone, then the rest would fall."

"Cut off the head and the body will fall!" Tito said.

"Who was the shooter?" Omar asked.

"His name is Lou. That's all I know," Tony replied.

The name drew a blank. No one knew who the hell he was, which made sense. Omar couldn't see a hitman who knew what they were capable of going up against them.

"Where do we find this Lou?"

"I don't know. All we have is a number. I page him and put in the number for what time I want to meet and he goes to our meeting spot at that time. We always meet up in the back of this building."

Will started to become nervous and jittery. He started to move around on the couch. Raul quickly moved in on him and that caught Tito's attention. Without even thinking, Tony grabbed one of the pistols he'd dropped and got off two shots at Tito. Omar quickly dove for cover. Raul didn't hesitate. He pulled the trigger and shot Will five times.

Tony's first shot missed Tito clearly, but the second grazed his side. The bullet spun him around. Tony quickly fired more shots, this time at Raul. By that time, Raul had already sought cover. Tony, however, was still on the floor out in the open. Tito quickly popped up and shot him in the chest. Tony dropped his pistol and tried to catch his breath. Blood started to come out of his mouth as he coughed. He could feel his life slipping away from him.

Tito walked up on Tony as he was gasping for air. He kicked Tony's gun away from him. Raul and Omar both got up, now that the coast was clear.

"Finish him and let's get out of here," Omar said.

Tito shot Tony in the crown of his head, ending his suffering. All of them started to make their way for the door.

"The number," Tito said.

"What number?" Omar asked.

"The hitman! He said he paged him; that's how he knew to meet them. Maybe we can use the number."

"How? He meets them around here. It's not like we can ambush him here. Not now!" Omar replied.

"I realize that but we still might be able to use it. Right now, this is the only lead we have to who killed Jose. Why disregard it? Why not use it, even if we have to later?"

Omar agreed. Tito patted Tony down, looking for his cell phone. He quickly went through it, looking for the name Lou.

"I found it," Tito said as he spotted the name. He clicked on the name to see the number. To his surprise, he knew the number well. Tito continued, "Oh shit! I can't believe it."

"What is it?" Omar questioned.

Tito walked over to Omar to show him the number. Omar looked at the phone.

"You've got to be kidding me!" Omar yelled. As Omar looked at the number, he felt so small. He felt like an idiot that he had never put two and two together. How did he miss it? He became filled with outrage. Tony and Carlos's motive was obvious; ambition. But betrayal could never be explained. Omar continued, "How is your side?"

"I'm good," Tito reassured Omar.

"Okay, let's get out of here. You know the next stop!"

18

Lisa followed closely behind Detective Peterson, making sure she didn't lose him. She made sure to stay three cars behind him. As Derrick had instructed, Detective Peterson was heading to their meeting spot. It was definitely Detective Peterson. Detective Peterson pulled into the parking lot of Safeway and then parked his car.

Lisa pulled into the parking lot and parked the car also. She made sure they had a good view of Detective Peterson. Derrick called Detective Peterson to give him his instructions. He instructed him to get out of the car and walk over to the post office. Derrick got out of the car and started to walk over to him.

Derrick walked right past Detective Peterson and into the post office. Detective Peterson stood there, waiting for his next move. He noticed Derrick when he walked by and noticed the resemblance, but couldn't think of from where. Derrick stood there, looking at Detective Peterson. He knew his next step, but his nerves were getting the best of him. Derrick realized that now was the time. He headed back to the front door toward Detective Peterson.

Detective Peterson pulled the picture he had taken from Derrick's apartment out of his pocket and looked at it. Now he knew exactly where he knew the passing man from. It was Derrick. Before he could turn to head into the post office, Derrick was already behind him with his gun in Detective Peterson's waist.

"Mr. Anderson?"

"Come on; let's go," Derrick instructed.

"Now, Mr. Anderson, don't do anything stupid that you'll regret," Detective Peterson said as he walked toward Lisa's car.

"Look, please stop talking and just walk. Hurry up!" Derrick replied.

They were quickly approaching the car. "Get in the front seat," Derrick told Detective Peterson once they reached the car. He did as Derrick told him. Derrick got into the backseat.

Lisa noticed Derrick had his gun pointed straight at Detective Peterson.

"Derrick, what are you doing? You didn't say anything about kidnapping him. You were supposed to be showing him the damn picture and that's it."

"Shut the hell up, Lisa! Damn! Just drive the car around back."

"Derrick," Lisa called his name again, hoping he'd come to his senses.

"Lisa, drive the damn car!" Derrick yelled back.

Lisa put the car in drive and did as Derrick had told her to do.

"Mr. Anderson, right now you're only a witness. You do not want to travel down this road and add criminal charges to it."

Derrick ignored Detective Peterson. Lisa pulled around to the back of the Safeway by the loading area.

"What now, Mr. Anderson? Now, what are you going to do?" Detective Peterson questioned.

"How do I know you didn't have anything to do with Thomas's murder? How do I know you aren't in on the whole damn thing?'

"You don't; you're going to have to trust me."

"Like earlier? I trusted you then, and was almost killed. I'm supposed to trust you now, too? I mean, don't you find it ironic that the exact day that I'm supposed to meet you, the same person who killed Jose Benitez shows up? To me, that's no coincidence. That is, unless you're a part of the entire scheme and now you're trying to cover up all your loose ends."

"So killing me will prove what exactly? Riddle me that," Detective Peterson replied.

"It won't prove anything but it would be one less person after my ass."

"You're right. It definitely will be one less person after you. The only problem with that is you would've gotten rid of the only person who's trying to help you and can save your black ass. Now, let's cut the bullshit! You know that I didn't have anything to do with whatever happened earlier and I damn sure didn't have anything to do with Benitez's murder."

Derrick's phone started to ring as he was thinking about what Detective Peterson had to say. It was his mother calling. She was probably worried sick about him. He normally talked to her at least once a day and hadn't spoken with her since everything had happened. He hit ignore on the phone. Now was not the time to explain everything to his mother.

"Derrick, I believe him. Come on, show him what we have so we can get out of here," Lisa said.

"Show me what? What is it?" Detective Peterson asked, wondering what Lisa was referring to.

"Earlier today in the mall, before he saw me, I took a picture of the killer with my phone. That way we don't need to do no photo lineup or anything. I can show you what he looks like and you can see if you can put a name to the face. After that, I'm out!"

Derrick took out his cell phone, pulled up the picture of the killer, and showed it to Detective Peterson. Detective Peterson couldn't believe what he was seeing.

"Are you sure this is the same person you saw kill Jose Benitez?" Detective Peterson asked.

"I'm positive and as you can see, he's also the same person who tried to kill me again earlier today when I was supposed to be meeting you."

Detective Peterson handed Derrick his phone back. He was at a loss for words. He knew that Derrick wasn't lying about what he was saying or what he had seen but still, something didn't see right. None of it made any sense. Derrick's phone started to ring again. It was his mother again. Usually, if he ignored one of her calls, she'd leave him a message to call her back. It must've been an emergency.

"Who is that?" Lisa questioned.

"It's my mother. I haven't talked to her since everything went down. She's probably worried sick. Hold on, I need to let her know that I'm aiight," Derrick replied as he was answering the phone.

"Derrick," Lisa said, trying to stop him.

"Hey, Ma. Look, I can't talk right now. I'm sorry that I haven't called you but I promise, I'll call you later on today to explain everything to you."

"I'm sorry, your mother can't come to the phone right now," a strange voice said.

"Who is this?" Derrick asked.

"You know exactly who it is. How long did you think it would be before I caught up with mommy dearest?"

"Look, please don't do anything to my mother. She has nothing to do with this. This is between you and me."

"Put the phone on speaker," Detective Peterson whispered to Derrick. Derrick did as he asked.

"She has everything to do with it. She'll make sure you do everything I say. Now get your ass over here and bring that bitch with you, too," the killer said.

Derrick quickly muted his phone.

"How does he know about me?" Lisa asked.

"What should I do?" Derrick asked.

"What choice is he leaving us? Tell him that you'll meet him," Detective Peterson replied.

Derrick took phone off of mute. "Okay, but what if I can't find her? She isn't with me right now. Plus, why do you need her? She didn't see anything and it's not like she knows anything. Like I told you, I'm the one you want."

"Look, I want both you and her here, and you better be coming alone. If I even think I see a cop, your mother is gone. I'll make sure it takes you months to find every piece of her body that I plant throughout the city."

"How do I know she's even alive? For all I know, you already killed her. I'm not doing a damn thing until you let me talk to her."

"You will do what I say," the killer repeated.

Derrick hung up the phone.

"What are you doing?" Detective Peterson asked. "You don't want to piss him off and make matters worse."

"If my mother is alive, he'll call back. I'm who he wants."

Derrick's phone started to ring as he predicted. He answered the phone.

"Hello…Derrick," he heard his mother say.

"Ma, are you okay? He hasn't hurt you, has he?"

"No, he hasn't. I'm alright; please just do whatever he says, Derrick."

"I'm going to get you out of this, I promise. I'll get you out of this, Ma," Derrick said. His mother didn't reply. "Hello? Hello, Ma?"

"Now you've talked to her. You know she's fine. How long she stays that way is solely up to you. You need to find that bitch and both of you get here," the killer said and hung up the phone.

Up until that point, Derrick had done fine, figuring out what moves to make, but now he was way in over his head. He was no longer in control of the situation. The killer had the one thing that meant the most to him in this world, his mom, and Derrick wasn't about to risk losing her.

Derrick aimed his gun at Detective Peterson again. "I'm sorry. You're only trying to help but this is where we draw the line. I've done all that I can do for you. Now, I have to take matters into my own hands. This is my mother we are talking about."

"If you go in there, all he's going to do is kill you, your mother, and your friend. What good would that do? I told you, let me help you," Detective Peterson pleaded.

"How? He's already said that if he sees you, my mother is gone. What more can we do? My hands are tied. I have to do exactly what he wants."

"Derrick, you are on your own. I'll be damned if I go and allow him to just kill me. I'm sorry, but I won't do it," Lisa said.

"I wasn't going to ask you to. You're getting out of the car with Detective Peterson. I'm the one he wants. He only asked for you because of earlier. He must've spotted you in the car but once he has me, he won't need anyone else," Derrick said to Lisa. He looked at Detective Peterson. "You've got what you need to find him. Please, do. Don't let me die for nothing."

"Derrick," Lisa pleaded.

"Come on now; y'all get out of the car. Please don't force my hand. I will use this thing if I have to."

"You and I both know you aren't, Mr. Anderson. Now if you want to go about it alone, that's fine. I can't stop you, but hear me out. The person who killed Jose Benitez and who has your mother is a cop. His name is Inspector Lewis. He's the secondary detective on this case, actually. I now know that isn't by coincidence either."

Derrick sat there in awe. He didn't know what to say. Detective Peterson continued, "Right now, he doesn't know that I've talked to you. He doesn't know that I know everything. I told you before, together we can bring him down and I meant that."

"How detective? Please tell me how?" Derrick asked.

"We go together. You have a key to your mother's house, don't you? Well, you go in the front door and I'll go in the back and together, we will bring him down. But if you go in there alone, he will certainly kill both you and your mother. That, I can't have. I will not allow that to happen; not on my watch."

"Derrick, please, listen to him. Let him help. What other choice do we have right now? He's telling the truth. You're worried about your mother but, without his help, your mother doesn't stand a chance. At least with his help, she has somewhat of a chance. We all do. Please, let him help, Derrick."

"Okay, fine, I'm in, but nothing can happen to my mother. I won't be able to live with myself if anything happens to her."

"Nothing's going to happen to anyone. We're all going to pull through this," Detective Peterson replied.

19

etective Peterson had been over the plan time and time again with Derrick. If he did things just how he asked, everything would go as he planned. Lewis wouldn't know what hit him and before he would have time to react, he'd already be in handcuffs. Everything wasn't as cut and dried for Derrick, though. He'd never been in a situation like this before. Not when his mother's and his life both rested on a plan that possibly couldn't work or possibly could backfire.

Derrick stopped at the bottom of the street and let Detective Peterson out of the car.

"Remember, do everything exactly like we planned. I'll be right there with you."

Detective Peterson got out of the car and made his way to the house on foot. Derrick drove off and headed to this mother's house. Once he was there, he parked in the driveway. Derrick said a silent prayer to himself. He didn't see how asking the Lord for a little extra help could hurt. Derrick got out of the car and walked up to the house. He put his key in the door and opened it.

The lights were off in the house.

"Ma," Derrick called out. There was no response. Derrick walked into the living room and saw his mother sitting there, tied up with tape over her mouth. Derrick ran over to her and removed the tape.

"Ma, are you alright?" Derrick asked.

"I'm fine, baby. I'm okay."

"I told you she'd be fine if you did what I said," Lewis said.

Derrick turned around and saw Lewis standing there with a gun aimed at him.

"Ma, I'm going to get you out of this," Derrick reassured her.

"Where is the bitch? I said that I wanted both of you here. Where is she?" Lewis asked.

"She's my insurance that you let my mother leave. You have me here. I'm the one you want. Once you let my mother go, I'll call her to come. Not a minute before or a minute after. You didn't think that I'd be all in and let you hold all the cards, did you?"

Lewis walked over to Derrick. "Either you call her, or I'll kill the both of you. I'll start with your mother first and make you watch every minute of it. Now call her and tell her to get her ass in here."

"She isn't out front. I told you, I wasn't going to be all in. I don't trust you! You let my mother go and I'll call her and tell her that it's okay for her to come. If not, then it'll just be the two of us."

Lewis started to get frustrated. He swung vigorously at Derrick. His punch connected to the back of Derrick's head as he tried to get out of the way of it. Derrick immediately fell to the floor. Lewis put his gun to Derrick's mother's head.

"Call her now, or I kill your mother," Lewis demanded.

"Go ahead; I'd love to see you explain our murders to the police. I've already told her that if she doesn't hear from me in ten minutes to go to the police and show them the picture that I took of you earlier. You see, I told you, there was no way I'd be all in. Now with both of us here, then you don't have to worry.

You'll have both witnesses and the only link to you. But you will let my mother go. So the choice is yours; you make the call."

Lewis didn't know if any of what Derrick had said was true. But if he did have a picture of him and now the girl had it, then his whole plan would crumble. There would be too much to try to explain and there was no guarantee whatever he came up with would be believable.

"Fine," Lewis said as he started to untie Derrick's mom.

Once she was totally untied, she ran over to Derrick to hug him.

"Come on, Ma, you've got to get out of here. I'll be aiight; trust me. Now go ahead and get out of here."

Derrick's mother gave him a kiss and did as he asked.

"I let the old bitch go; now call her," Lewis demanded.

The look on Derrick's face said he didn't appreciate Lewis calling his mother a bitch.

"If you didn't have that gun, I'd show you just who the bitch really is."

"Yeah, is that so? I hear you. Now do us both a favor and call her. I don't need to hear your empty-ass threats; you and I both know you won't do shit but what you've continued to do: run."

Derrick did as promised. He took out his phone to call Lisa.

"Yeah, she is out the door. You can come in now," Derrick said before he hung up the phone. Derrick went over to the couch and sat down. Surprisingly, he seemed more at-ease. "Why did you do it?"

"That's none of your concern. All you need to worry about is her getting here before I lose my patience with you," Lewis replied.

"So what are we going to do, sit here and look at one another? You've turned my life upside down. I've earned the right to know why."

"You were in the wrong place at the wrong time. This had nothing to do with you, but hey, you saw me put two in Jose and left me no choice. I couldn't leave you alive after that."

"You could've easily let me be. I told you, I would've disappeared. I wouldn't have been trouble for you or anyone else."

"I couldn't risk it. Maybe if it wasn't Jose, then maybe I could've considered it, but I couldn't risk Omar finding out anything about his nephew. It wouldn't have been in my best interest."

"So what are you going to do now?"

"Don't be naïve. You know exactly what choices and options I have left. You've only left me with one. Look at it this way; at least you were able to save your mother's life."

"How do I know that? She's a witness, just like I am. How do I know that you won't go back after her? I'm not assured of anything," Derrick replied.

"It was never about your mother. I might be a lot of things, but that coldhearted, I'm not. I have a mother myself and if anyone did anything to her, I'd lose my mind. I do have some type of code. But I had to use her, in order to get you here. Plus, who is your mother going to go to, the police? I'm not worried about them; it's not like she'll ever see me again anyway. I'll take my chances with the police sketch artist."

There was a knock at the front door. Lewis got up to look out the window. He didn't see any extra cars in front of the house.

"Go see who is at the door," Lewis told Derrick. Derrick got up from the couch and went to the front door. He looked out of the peephole.

"There isn't anyone there," Derrick replied.

"I heard a damn knock on the door," Lewis said. "Open the door. Look outside. Maybe you can't see them."

Derrick opened the door. There was no one standing there. Derrick looked back at Lewis. He opened the door a little wider.

Yet still, there was no one there. Lewis moved back from the door as Derrick appeared to close the door shut. He motioned for Derrick to go back into the living room. Derrick went and sat back down on the couch.

"So what are you going to do if Omar ever finds out about you?" Derrick asked.

"That's one thing I don't have to worry about, now that I have you."

"Are you sure about that?" Omar asked as he walked into the room.

Lewis couldn't believe his eyes. He quickly tried to regroup himself.

"Hey, Omar, what are you doing here?"

"Funny, I could ask you the same thing, but I already know the answer to that question, so why bother?"

"What are you talking about, Omar?"

"Lewis, please don't insult my intelligence. The only thing that I want to know is, was the money worth it?" Omar questioned.

"Omar, I don't know what he has told you—"

Omar quickly cut him off. "I've already told you, please don't insult me. He hasn't told me anything. You told me everything. You see, your little friends Tony and Carlos are the ones who gave you up. So I ask you, was my nephew worth it?"

Lewis knew that nothing he said would get him out of the situation he was in. He was so shook when Omar first came in, he didn't even notice that he was alone. Tito or Omar's driver were always close by, but Lewis knew that Omar's driver was dead so that meant that Tito must've been somewhere close by but where? If he wasn't already there, then he must've been on the way. Lewis turned his pistol on Omar.

Omar didn't back down; instead, he cracked a smile. He had Lewis exactly where he wanted him. Omar walked toward the couch where Derrick was sitting. Derrick was on edge. He started to question Detective Peterson's plan. Being a witness to Lewis killing Jose was how he had gotten into this situation in the first place. Witnessing Omar kill Lewis wouldn't make matters any better. Omar looked at Derrick and then turned back to Lewis.

"Who's your friend?" Omar asked, referring to Derrick.

"I'm not with him. He was trying to kill my mother," Derrick quickly replied. He didn't want Omar thinking he was associated with Lewis in any way.

"Both of you shut the fuck up! I need to think," Lewis said.

"About what, Lewis? What is there for you to think about? There's nowhere you can go that I won't find you. Your biggest mistake was that you should've killed me instead of Jose; I'm going to make sure you suffer," Omar said with a stern look on his face.

"Don't tempt me. I can take care of that right now, if you like."

"Is that right?" Omar asked as he started to move toward Lewis. "Well, come on then. What are you waiting for? Stop wasting my time and get it over with. Regardless, whether I'm dead or alive, you won't make it to your next birthday. That, I can guarantee. So come on and stop wasting my time and do it if you're going to."

Lewis didn't respond. He was hoping that Omar didn't call his bluff. Omar sensed the panic in Lewis's eyes.

"What are you waiting on? I'm right here. Just like Jose was. It shouldn't be a problem. Kill me," Omar said.

Lewis's attention was so squarely on Omar that he didn't even notice Tito coming up behind him. Derrick's eyes grew big but Lewis saw nothing. The cold barrel on the back of his head regained his attention. Lewis knew that Tito couldn't have been far, but as Omar was pressuring him, he had become discombobulated and had forgotten all about Tito. Tito reached around and took Lewis's pistol out of his hand.

Omar walked up to Lewis and then knocked him on the floor with a single punch. Tito noticed Derrick sitting there.

"What about him?" Tito asked.

"My friend, you said he tried to kill your grandmother, right?" Omar asked.

"No, it was my mother. He held my mother hostage," Derrick replied.

"I do apologize. Come on over here and get your revenge."

As tempting as Omar's offer was, Derrick didn't want any part of what was about to take place. All he wanted to do was to get out of there with his life and he'd be fine with that.

"That's okay. I'd much rather like to go check on her."

"I don't know if I can help you with that. Now, if you want to get in some punches beforehand, that I definitely can help you out with," Omar replied.

Lewis was trying to crawl away while Omar talked to Derrick. Omar stepped on the back of Lewis's neck and pushed him down to the ground. Tito waved his gun at Derrick as if to tell him to come on. Derrick didn't move. He knew that wasn't the smartest of moves. However, he didn't want any part of their plan.

"D.C. Police, everybody down on the ground now!" officers yelled as they stormed the house.

Tito quickly put his hands up in the air. Omar didn't move as officers had guns pointed at him. One of the officers noticed Lewis on the ground. They picked him up off the floor. Detective Peterson walked into the room.

"Thank God, y'all got here. They were trying to kill us," Lewis said.

Detective Peterson surveyed the room. He looked at Omar, then Tito, and lastly Lewis.

"My, my, my, what do we have here? Mr. Benitez, I told you to stay out of my investigation but yet, I find you here."

Detective Peterson walked over to pat him down. To Detective Peterson's surprise, Omar was unarmed. Tito wasn't as lucky. He not only had his gun, but he still had Lewis's police-issued gun as well.

"Man, I'm so glad to see you, Pete. You just don't know," Lewis said.

"Don't be too happy because you'll be joining your little friends. Charles Lewis, you're under the arrest for the murder of Jose Benitez. You have the right to remain silent. Anything you say can and will be used against you in a court of law. You have the right to speak to an attorney. If you cannot afford an attorney, one will be appointed for you. Do you understand these rights as I have explained them to you?" Detective Peterson said to Lewis as he handcuffed them.

"You've got to be kidding me. Murder? I didn't murder no damn Benitez? I'm D.C. police."

Detective Peterson took his badge. "You are far from one of us. Now do you understand these rights as I've explained them to you?"

"Yeah, I understand them just like I also understand that you don't have anything on me."

Detective Peterson took a recorder out of his pocket and pressed the PLAY button.

"You've turned my life upside down. I've earned the right to know why," Derrick's voice said on the recorder.

"You were just in the wrong place at the wrong time. This had nothing to do with you, but hey, you saw me put two in Jose and left me no choice. I couldn't leave you alive after that," Lewis had replied.

Detective Peterson stopped the tape.

"Yeah, I have enough," Detective Peterson replied. He turned to the other officers. "Get them out of here."

Omar was the only one not in handcuffs. The officer looked at Detective Peterson. "What about him?" Omar wasn't carrying a weapon and didn't exactly say what he was going to do to Lewis so Detective Peterson knew the evidence against Omar was very slim; however, he didn't care.

"Arrest him, too," he replied.

Omar cracked a smile. "You and I both know the charges won't last. I can do the day or two away."

"You might be right, but I promised you that if you got in the way of my investigation, it would end with you in cuffs just like I told you that I'd get your nephew's killer. I'm a man of my word, Mr. Benitez."

"That you are, detective. That you are! Good move," Omar said as he put his hands behind his back.

The officer cuffed him and took him out also. Detective Peterson walked over to Derrick.

"Are you okay?"

"I'm fine. I want to get out of here," Derrick replied.

"I can understand that. Lisa and your mother are outside waiting for you."

Derrick and Detective Peterson started walking toward the front door. Derrick stopped.

"Detective…"

Detective Peterson stopped and looked up at him.

"Thanks for keeping your word to me, and also proving that I could trust you," Derrick said as he extended his hand.

Detective Peterson shook Derrick's extending hand. "I told you, before anything, I'm a man first and a man stands behind his word."

20

Two weeks had gone by since the arrests. Detective Peterson was going through some reports on his desk. He'd taken a brief and well-deserved vacation after he'd solved Josc Benitez's murder. Once he returned, he was shocked to find out that Omar was still in jail. That didn't make any sense being as there was no real concrete evidence against him. He should've been held a couple of hours, if that.

"Hello, detective," a voice said behind Detective Peterson. He turned around to see Derrick standing there.

"Hey there, Mr. Anderson, how have you been?"

"I can't complain. I'm about to get out of town and check out some apartments in Charlotte. I thought that I'd peek my head in on you and see how things were."

"Charlotte, huh? So you're going to skip town and move?"

"Yeah, I've had about enough of D.C. I need to go somewhere more my speed; plus, we have family in North and South Carolina. It's time for a change."

"We? Is Lisa going with you?"

"No, my mother and me. I haven't spoken to Lisa in a few days. She was also thinking about relocating, but I don't know if she'll actually do it."

"What? You're leaving your girl?" Detective Peterson asked.

"Oh, you thought she and I were together? No, she was Thomas's girlfriend. We were all together when, well, you know, everything happened. I couldn't leave her to fend for herself out here."

"I can respect that. So what brings you by?"

"I wanted to see if you were going to need me to testify. I tried calling you and they told me that you'd be back today. I figured that I'd come in and ask."

"I doubt the district attorney needs you since Lewis confessed on tape, but I'm sure she can use you to add an extra nail in the coffin, if you're up to it." Detective Peterson paused. "Actually, what am I thinking? You actually witnessed the murder so, without a doubt, you'll need to testify. An eyewitness trumps taped evidence any day."

They both grinned.

"I've been thinking a lot about it and Thomas would want me to see things through. It'll bring closure. Yeah, I definitely want to, but what about Omar and his friend?"

"You don't have to worry about Tito Vasquez. He had the weapons on him. The officers would've testified against him as to what they found on him but that's a mute point now. He pled out last week, I hear. They gave him seven years. As for Omar, he's still being held; he'll be out soon, but he still isn't anything to worry about. He knows you can't hurt him and plus, all he really ever wanted was justice for his nephew and he got that."

"Cool, well, let me get up out of here. My mom's waiting in the car," Derrick said.

Detective Peterson shook his hand. "Tell her that I said hello and you drive safe now."

"No problem," Derrick said as he started to head to the door. He turned back toward Detective Peterson. "I've told you this before but thanks for keeping your word. I don't think that I'd be here now, if you didn't." Derrick then left out of the room.

Detective Peterson sat back down in his chair and couldn't help but smile. He felt a sense of accomplishment. It felt good to be appreciated. He replayed all that had transpired over the past couple of weeks and could only imagine all that Derrick had gone through, and then he remembered Omar. He still couldn't figure out why he was still being held in custody. There was no way a judge had denied bail so he should've long been out. He couldn't even remember the official charge they had given him.

Detective Peterson grabbed his keys and went up to the desk sergeant.

"I'll be back. I'm going to head down to the D.C. Jail."

"What's in D.C. Jail? You just got back off vacation; don't you want to take it easy?" the desk sergeant asked.

"I'm cool; I have some questions that I need answered, is all. I should be back in about an hour or two. I might grab something to eat on the way back. If anything comes up, hit me on the radio."

✠ ✠ ✠

Detective Peterson sat at the interview table, waiting for the prisoner to come into the room. The guard opened the door and in walked Omar. He couldn't help but smile once he saw him.

"Detective, to what do I owe this pleasure?"

"I should be asking you that question. You and I both know you're only in here for a reason and if it's for what I think it's for, then you and I need to talk."

"Detective, you truly worry too much. Some things are much simpler than what they seem. Maybe you should talk to your district attorney. I'm being held until they can transfer me into federal custody. It has nothing to do with your case," Omar replied coolly.

"Is that right? Because if I find out you or any of your followers come anywhere near Derrick Anderson, I'll hunt you down, and coming back here will be the least of your worries. He is not to be touched. Is that clear?" Detective Peterson threatened.

"Who is Derrick Anderson?"

"Now you want to play dumb; don't test me!"

"Look, detective, I admire a man of passion like you. It's very refreshing. You don't see many in your line of work as passionate as you are."

Detective Peterson stood up and walked over to Omar. He whispered in his ear, "I've already proven once before to be a man of my word. Do you really want to test me again? Stay away from Derrick Anderson."

"Detective, you have proven to me to be a man of honor. I appreciate what you've done in regards to my nephew. I have no need for Mr. Anderson. You now have my word. No one from my camp will ever come in contact with him or his family."

"Are you trying to play word games with me? No one will come in contact with him. That isn't saying anything to me."

"Detective, please rest assured that no one will touch Mr. Anderson. He is safe. He has nothing to worry about. Is that better? You have my word on that. Now go ahead and enjoy the press you've gotten on my arrest. I'm actually enjoying myself in prison. It's like a mini-vacation so to speak. We all need one of those, right?" Omar said before he burst into laughter.

"I never knew prison could be a vacation."

"It's not but, in my line of work, any time away from the streets is a vacation. I'm getting good exercise and peace of mind. I actually was in the middle of something before they told me that I had a visitor."

Detective Peterson headed toward the door. "For your sake, I hope you're a man of your word. Enjoy the rest of your vacation stay," he said and then exited the room.

"It won't be for long; once I complete my unfinished business," Omar said as the guard entered the room to escort him back to his cell.

They walked down the corridor and into another room. Tito was inside the room with three other guards. Tito walked up to him, whispered something into his ear and then moved aside. Omar walked further into the room to a man lying on the floor.

"Come on, my friend; you're taking all the fun out of this," Omar said to him. The man turned over. He had been badly beaten.

"Omar, please," Lewis said, pleading for the torture to end.

"Please, my ass! I told you, I was going to enjoy every minute of this. You should've known there was no place that you could go that I wouldn't reach out and touch you."

Lewis started coughing. Omar and Tito had taken turns beating him, burning him, and doing anything that came to mind for the past four days. Omar gave one of the guards a look.

"Come on, fellas; it's lunchtime. Mr. Benitez, we'll be back in about two hours for roll call. Do you need anything?" the guard asked.

"No, my friend; I'm good," Omar replied.

The guards each turned and headed out the door, leaving Omar and Tito to have their way with Lewis.

"Now, where were we?" Omar said as he took a ready-made jail cell knife out of his pocket.

ABOUT THE AUTHOR

Harell, aka Harold L. Turley II, is a performance poet and the author of *Love's Game, Confessions of a Lonely Soul, Born Dying*, and *My Darkest Hour.* He is a contributing author to *Nikki Turner Presents Backstage.* He lives with his children in Maryland. Visit the author at www.haroldlturley.com or on Facebook.

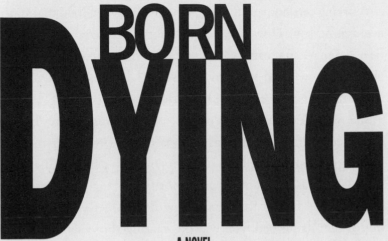
THE MAKING OF MONEY GREEN
CHAPTER 1

"Nate," a woman yelled from the other room in the house.
"Nate, get up! You are going to be late for school!"

Nate was dead tired from the night before and school was the
last thought on his mind. He didn't feel like budging. Usually

his mother would give him a courtesy wake-up call, and then she would head straight for her bedroom where the comfort of her bed awaited her after a long night at work.

Working ten-hour shifts for Telnex Wireless will do that to the average person. However, Nate's mother realized she couldn't be average when it came to her son, especially after she found out about his newfound habit to skip school. At that point, average could no longer be a part of her title.

She was determined to make sure he was where he was supposed to be when he was supposed to be, whether it meant missing a couple of minutes or hours of sleep per day. She didn't care. Nate was her number one priority.

"Nathaniel Donte Rodgers, if you do not get your skinny ass out of that damn bed, you will be wearing those same sheets to your funeral next week," she said as she shook his bed to make sure he'd get up.

"Damn, Ma, I'm up!"

"Excuse you? Who the hell do you think you are talking to? You want to cuss in this house, then you need to go through nine months of pregnancy, forty-six hours of labor, and pay the household bills by yourself. When you do all that, then you can cuss in this house. Other than that you will respect me and my house or I will knock your ass on the floor. Are we clear?"

The smirk that painted Nate's face showed that he understood his mother completely but also took part of what was said as a joke. His mother never had a problem playing tough, but when it came time to lay down the law physically, she was nothing but a pussycat.

"Boy, if you don't wipe that damn smirk off your face…"

Nate cut her off, "I know, I know. You are going to knock me into the middle of next week."

He couldn't help but laugh after repeating a saying his mother said over and over again.

"I'm sorry, Ma, it will never happen again. I was half asleep."

"What have I told you about saying you are sorry? I didn't have a 'sorry' child."

"Excuse me, I meant, I apologize. Now if you don't mind, Mother, can you excuse me so I can get dressed?"

"Boy, please, I've seen what you have. I'm the one who diapered that little thing of yours."

"Ma, there is nothing *little* about my thing."

Now she'd found something to be amused about. She broke out into laughter.

"Child, please, at fourteen years old, everything is little on you but your heart. That is the only thing big a fourteen-year-old can have. Now let's get ready for school so you can continue to expand your mind."

He started to get out of the bed.

"I'll let your little comment slide since you are my mother and I love you, but don't let it happen again. I know a couple of girls who would disagree with you, though."

That caught Nate's mother off guard and now she was definitely intrigued.

"Oh really, is that right? You keep digging yourself a hole deeper and deeper and you don't even know it. Sooner or later, it's going to be so deep you'll never get out of it. "

"It was a joke, Ma. I didn't mean anything by it. I was just pushing your buttons."

She wasn't buying it. "I bet. I know if you are dumb enough to be poking that thing around you need to be at least smart enough to know you need to be wearing a condom as well. Kids these days want to grow up so fast but when they have to face consequences for their actions, then that's when they want to be kids again."

"Ma, come on! It's really not that serious. It was a joke."

"Don't 'come on, Ma' me and don't brush off what I'm saying, either. I'm serious. It's too much shit traveling around out here in these streets and I don't need you bringing it into this house. It used to be all you had to worry about was getting a woman pregnant, but now you have to worry about saving your life."

Nate knew the only way this conversation would ever end would be if he ignored her. He couldn't assure her that he was using protection because then she'd want to know more about his sex life such as when, where, and with whom. If he said he wasn't using protection she'd question as to why not, run down all the possible diseases he could contract, then would start up with the when, where, and with who.

There was no way she'd buy he wasn't sexually active. Then she'd go into her "don't lie to me" speech and the morning would become even longer. Nate decided to do the only thing he could, get ready for school. He just looked at her with his hazel eyes and kept his mouth closed.

"Do you hear me talking to you?" she questioned.

He nodded trying not to be totally disrespectful.

She became frustrated. "It's too early in the morning to be going through this and I'm too tired. Get your ass up and get ready for school."

Nate knew that wasn't the last of that conversation but at least it was for today. His mother finally left the room. Nate decided to make a mental note to get an alarm clock later that day to make sure she didn't have to wake him up anymore and to avoid these types of talks. He thought it was cool being able to talk to your mother, but you didn't want to talk to her about every damn thing. He headed for his closet to pull out an outfit to wear to school. He grabbed a pair of blue jeans and a white T-shirt, nothing special. Nate never saw fit to be flashy. It only brought more attention to yourself.

By the time he got out of the shower and dressed, his mother was fast asleep. He walked into her room and put the covers over top of her, then gave her a kiss on the forehead. He made sure to put two hundred in her purse and hoped she would use it for something regarding the house.

Nate made it a habit to slip money into his mother's purse. He just made sure to put it in the middle of whatever cash she had in her wallet so it didn't stand out. It obviously was working because up to date, she had never questioned him about anything. He knew if she had any clue about what he was doing, then she would have questioned him to the end trying to find out where the money came from. However, those were answers that he knew she would never be ready to deal with.

CHAPTER 2

Nate walked into Oxon Hill High School in Oxon Hill, Maryland, and headed straight for his locker. His day began with English, geometry, and finally Spanish before lunch. He couldn't stand his class schedule. If it were up to him, PE would have been stuck somewhere in between that load.

To his surprise, O'Neal was standing at his locker waiting for Nate. O'Neal and Nate went back since pee-wee football. They were best friends and business partners. He was never real big on school so whenever anyone saw him there, it was shocking.

O'Neal was a year older but because of his lack of enthusiasm for education, he was held back and they both were in the same grade.

"Are you ready to break out?" he asked.

"We don't have a job?"

"What's your point, Nate?"

"My point is I can't mess with it today. It's one thing to roll and make some extra change. But it's a whole different ball game to fuck up in school, cause my mother to get suspicious to what I'm doing, and eventually mess with my paper trail, all because I wanted to do was break camp just for the hell of it."

"Keep your pager on then because you know how Chico is. When work needs to be put in, he doesn't factor your English test into consideration." O'Neal extended his hand to give Nate some dap. "I might stick around for a few to try to catch up with the shortie we bumped in to last night. If not, I'll just catch up with you around the way."

"That sounds like a plan."

Nate grabbed his books out of his locker and headed to class. School really was just something to do to pass time to him. He always felt as if there was nothing being taught to him that he'd use in the future. Only the school of hard knocks provided you with the lesson that would be needed for the streets.

Nate was a momma's boy, though and an education was to please her so he did. He'd do anything to make that woman happy. She took things very hard when she lost Nate's father to drugs in the '80s. Nate didn't want to put his mother through that horror again.

Instead, he did whatever it took to make sure he got acceptable grades. He didn't want to overdo things and stand out, either. If so, then the bar would be raised and his mother would grow to expect it. So he made sure to sprinkle in a couple of A's or B's along with a few D's on there as well. That way, there was always something he could improve upon in her eyes.

✪ ✪ ✪

Nate walked into the cafeteria after his brutal morning schedule ready to relax. To his surprise, O'Neal was still at school. There was no way he'd ever leave and come back all in one day. If he was out, you wouldn't see him anymore until you met up with him after school around the neighborhood.

There was only one thing that could have kept him at school and she was standing right next to him as he was trying to throw on the charm. Nate walked over to the back of the cafeteria where they were standing. O'Neal was in prime form. Pussy was always on his mind. That, if not his temper, would be his biggest downfall.

"What's good? I thought you were breaking camp earlier. Why the sudden change of heart?" Nate asked O'Neal even though he knew the answer. O'Neal shot him a look as if to say, *Stop frontin' like you don't already know.*

"I had some things I needed to take care of first. Have you met Nikki?"

"Naw, not formally, but I've seen her around before. You live in Forest Heights, right?"

"Damn, you stalking me or something?" she said defensively.

Nate quickly became defensive too. She was cute but far from his taste. Part of him took her remark as an insult. What need would he have to stalk her?

"Bitch, please! Don't flatter yourself because it's definitely not that serious!" Nate snapped back.

O'Neal put his hand over his head knowing the conversation from that point on was going nowhere but downhill.

"Who the fuck are you calling a bitch?"

"Calm down, boo! He didn't mean it like that," O'Neal said, trying to defuse the situation.

"Y'all niggas must have me twisted if you think I'm just going to sit here and let you talk to me any ole way. You best believe someone will be addressing this shit later on," she said, then stormed off before either of them could reply.

They both knew what she meant but it wasn't fazing either of them. The damage had already been done and when it came time to bump heads with them Forest Heights niggas, they'd be more than ready.

"Damn, nigga, when are you going to learn to control your mouth? You can't just say whatever comes to mind, especially when it's going to interfere with my action."

Nate couldn't help but laugh. O'Neal never let anything come between him and some action unless it was money.

"My bad. I didn't mean to throw a monkey wrench in your plans, seriously. But Slim came out the mouth wrong with that dumb shit and she needed to be put in her place quick. Don't fake! What do I look like stalking somebody, let alone her ass of all people?"

O'Neal found that very funny. "I was stalking her ass, though. Why didn't you tell me last night you knew where Slim stayed? I could have used that information."

"For what? I knew you'd find a way to catch up with her on your own and not look like you were pressed. Be honest, how does it look, you are never around Forest Heights, you don't live around there, but just happened to be around there to get at Slim out of the blue. That's some pressed shit. There is nothing original about that. Naw, you needed to catch up with her at school or wherever and then play your hand."

"Yeah, you right. Damn, it's about that time, though. We need to get up out of here."

"For what? I know you aren't tripping off that bullshit-ass threat."

"Come on now, you should know me better than that. When have I ever run from a fight? We have to be out because we have a meeting with Chico. He hit me up this morning."

Nate was dumbfounded but knew not to ask any questions. Chico was the one putting money in his pockets so if he called a meeting, Nate was definitely going to be in attendance.

"Did he say what it was about?"

"No, and I really didn't want to know, either. The only thing I needed to know was bread and he will be providing that, so I'm good."

O'Neal turned toward the double doors leading outside and headed through them. Nate wasn't too far behind him. The way the school was built, the cafeteria was at the front of the school and led straight to the parking lot where the school buses dropped off and picked up students.

Usually there were security guards out there but they were only there as props. They broke up the occasional fight here and there but that was about it. They didn't give a damn who left school early nor why. Half the time, they were trying to get the high school girls to leave early with them for some lunchtime fun.

Chico's black Lincoln Town Car pulled up at the bottom of the steps in the parking lot. We headed straight for it.

"What's going on, Chico?" O'Neal said the minute he got in the car.

"Hurry up and close the door. I have business to attend to."

Nate cut straight through the chase.

"How do we factor into these business plans?"

Chico found Nate's bluntness amusing.

"Always the straight shooter, huh, Nate? I like that."

Chico was a small-time dealer under the Cardoza crime family umbrella. Anyone who knew anything knew Mario Cardoza was the man to know in these streets. He held the power in D.C., and Chico was Nate's steppingstone up the ladder to the main man. O'Neal was only along for the small-time paper they were making.

To a couple of fourteen- and sixteen-year-olds, six hundred a week was a lot of money, especially to only be runners. Nate wasn't satisfied with that, though. No, he had bigger plans. He just needed the right avenue to make them happen. He was a firm believer that time and patience would open all the doors to anything they desired. You just had to wait your full course and that was something he was determined to do.

"Chico, my style will never change. I'm always going to be about that paper."

"Well, little homie, if you handle this job right, you will do just that. I've got something new for the both of you. Are you game?"

"Is money green?"